C000185783

GUNMASTER

Mason Price knew but one road—the way of the gunborn. He knew but one creed—the law of the bullet. He carried six dead men in each of his guns—and a star for himself to live by.

So where others built a town, Mason Price built its boothill. Where others made war, he made peace—with lead! He rode alone, as killers must, driven by an inner voice that whispered "The grass is always greener—on the other side of Hell!"

GUNMASTER

Ford Pendleton

GUNSMOKE

First published by Robert Hale, Ltd.

This hardback edition 2003
by Chivers Press
by arrangement with
Golden West Literary Agency

ISBN 0 7540 8221 0

British Library Cataloguing in Publication Data available.

Printed and bound in Great Britain by
Antony Rowe Ltd, Chippenham, Wiltshire

GUNMASTER

1

Standing fixed in the shadows of the saloon entrance, in this desert cowtown of Vale, watching an almost empty street, he remembered Bodie on the roaring nights of its wildcat boom. He had the same sense of submerged violence about to erupt, reading it in the vague mutterings of sound coming from the riotous shadows of the streets — he was a man attuned to violence. His name was Mason Price, and a ready anger and suspicion were the emotions that ruled his life. In this moment of total keenness he was feeling a little of each.

Something was up, yet all he saw at the moment was the man who a while ago had been standing before the dimly lighted window of a millinery store. Even as he watched, the light beyond the glass went out. That meant nothing, until he heard a muted cry — at the sound the man ducked under the hitch rail, went up on a streetside horse and rode into the shadows. Something in his actions betrayed a tight urgency.

Price moved. A lookout on the street meant the back of the building bore watching. Within seconds a slot across the thoroughfare had swallowed him. He had no clear reason for believing that Vale pertained to his mission in Snake Bend — a town farther up — other than rumors he had heard. But his suspicions grew stronger.

Pausing between the buildings in the rear, his first glance showed him another mounted man, with two saddled horses near him. A third man, on the ground, was in a lively strug-

7

gle with someone. The rider reached over and swung up
the gun he held.

"Let me slug her, Montana!" he grated. "She ain't gonna
come peaceful. I better buffalo her and you can tie her on."

The man on the ground panted to his victim, "You're
taking a little ride with us, honey. When he hears about it,
your killer brother will come outta hidin' real quick!"

Still swallowed in the shadows, Price felt gun grips
against the flats of his hands. The deadly, impersonal re-
action to violence tongued along his nerves like a fuse
burning toward dynamite. He spoke quietly, yet his voice
stabbed through the night. "Let go of her, damn you, and
stand back!"

Knowing beforehand that it wouldn't be enough, he
moved then, both guns out and roaring and heard the split-
ting roll of sound and saw the gun fly useless from the
rider's hand. With a wild, panicked curse the man named
Montana swung the woman between himself and Price.

Price fired, and Montana's hat was gone from his head.
The woman used that split second of confusion to break
loose and start toward Price.

"My next slug'll chew flesh," Price said as softly as he
had spoken before. "Lady, do you want to bring charges
against them?"

"No," she said in a torn gasp. "It — wouldn't do any
good."

"Then drift," Price said to the men, "and make it now."

The man named Montana stood steady for the space of
a slow breath, while the mounted man massaged his hand
and cursed softly. Then Montana walked over to a rider-
less horse and went up. Leading the mount intended for the
woman, the two rode out.

"Are you all right, ma'am?" Price asked.

"Yes."

"Where do you live?"

"In there." She nodded toward the rear door of the millinery store.

Shouts bucketed on the street. With the shooting over, investigators were willing to venture forth. Price didn't want to see them, to advertise until he had to do it that his guns had gone to work on the Oregon desert. It would be time enough when he pinned on the badge in Snake Bend — the country was unfamiliar to him.

"We'd better get out of here," he murmured. "Mind asking me in, ma'am?"

She hesitated, then turned. Her voice had sounded young, and she looked young in the starshine. He followed her across a weedy yard, up steps to a stoop. She paused again with her hand on the door knob, looking up at him and probably seeing nothing reassuring in the obscure light. Then she opened the door and stepped through.

Price thumbed a match afire, saw a lamp and lighted the wick. She was truly a girl, he saw, with tousled fair hair and with doubt showing very plainly in her brown, steady eyes. The room was austere, living quarters behind the millinery store, he judged, but it looked comfortable and neat.

"I don't know how you happened along," she said, "but thanks. They'd have laid me cold in a minute. They're — ruthless."

"Thought I heard you cry out," Price said vaguely. He never tried to explain how a man living by the gun grew so sensitive his intuitions were sometimes a burden. He had no wish to have this girl think him a freak.

She said, "You probably did. That Montana came into my shop and asked to see a present for a little girl. I was showing him some bonnets I'd made up when he grabbed me and blew out the lamp. I managed to yell before he got his hand over my mouth. That was what you heard and all that saved me."

"You knew them, ma'am?"

She shook her head. "I know who they are — I know who sent them and why." Yet she did not go on to explain.

"I heard some mention," Price said dryly, "of your brother."

"What you heard was a lie," she said. "My brother is not a killer." She stared at him in mounting suspicion. "Who are you, mister?"

"I'm Mason Price. I came across the desert from the railroad in Winnemucca. On my way to Snake Bend."

"You're not that Bodie gunman!" she gasped.

"I was Bodie's marshal." Price's voice grew tart.

"And you're going to Snake Bend," she said bitterly, "which means you'll work for Bent Shipstead. Everybody knows the old marshal was killed on his orders so he could put his own man on the job."

"I had a letter from Shipstead," Price admitted. "I don't know a thing about the old marshal, but if I take the job I'll be nobody's man."

"I believe that, of course," she said coldly. "But thanks for the help, even if Shipstead's going to be annoyed when he hears you gave it. Now, good night."

He stared at her, then nodded and went out, using the back door.

The curious had cleared out — the street was once more deserted. He thought a little sourly of the girl. Then dis-

missed her. He had had good women turn on him before
when they learned who and what he was. She had her
right to her feelings, he supposed — his gun was for sale.

The clerk on the desk at the Malheur Hotel was a wispy
oldster. He wore a sociable look as he laid out Price's
room key and asked, "What was the ruckus out there?"

Price shrugged, asked, "Who runs that little hat store
down the sidewalk?"

"Why, that's Hester Carson. A real nice gal."

"She alone?" Price asked idly.

"Well, she's got a brother," the clerk said, with hesita-
tion. "Nice boy, too, and doin' fine drivin' cattle to the
plains. But Will's a ringy cuss. She is, too, for that matter.
He got into trouble and had to pack his trunk."

"What kind of trouble?"

"Killed a man. First gun ruckus he was ever in, too, and
the setup didn't fit him atall. Couple of hombres who seen
it looks like they're right — and that's all I know."
it claim it was pure murder. They way Will lit his shuck,

Picking up his key, Price went on up the stairs, thinking
that Carson must not have packed his trunk very full or
run very far. He had heard Montana say that taking Carson's sister into their hands would bring him out of hiding
fast. They seemed to know that Carson was holed up somewhere in the surrounding country. They were anxious to
get hold of him for some reason, an urge natural in a lawman, but a little odd in them.

Hester Carson had implied that the pair worked for Shipstead. That was queer indeed, for Price had gathered that
the man was a sort of Jim Hill, come to this Snake River
cow country to help develop it, now that a railroad was
coming. But it was not Price's way to side with factions;

his interest lay solely in what he was hired to do.

He had left his lamp burning, as he always did, and could see its reassuring light in the crack under the door. Yet he entered the room warily. He made sure the blind was still drawn the way he had left it, and relocked the door slowly, deliberately, not daring to grow absentminded about it. Then he took off his hat and coat.

It was not to relax. There was still a hard set to his rough-cut face, and restlessness in his wide-set, black eyes. He flexed meaty shoulders, working the night's tension out of them, and out of his lean, hard middle. Lastly, he drew his guns.

The guns were worn-handled Colt .45's and for a moment he worked with them, spinning and rolling the emptied pieces and at times tossing them and changing hands. There was nothing pretentious about that, for it was needful to maintain the timing, rhythm and balance of the hands by which he stayed alive. Nor were the two guns vainglorious. They assured him of fire-power when he needed it, and the need came frequently.

Satisfied with the supple speed of his hands and arms, he reloaded his guns, finished undressing and went to bed. Even though his body settled onto the hard mattress, the tensions did not leave him at once. Those of the mind were hardest to loosen, held by the rutted thinking on which his life depended. There was so much a man dared not forget.

It was in the twilight zone between wakefulness and sleep that Price got closest to his inner self. Then emotion and thought and body energies ran aimlessly together. Then it was that he felt his only fear, counterbalanced by anger. Nearly always, then, his mind went back.

She was nineteen, dark, pretty, a hundred pounds and five feet tall. He was twenty — how many years ago? He could just count them on the fingers of hands since turned deadly. Kitty Oline, stepping from a mercantile into sudden gunfire on the street, to drop with a bullet in her brain.

His anger — his lust for law — had been born then. They drove him still, each time he drew his guns.

The fear that he had always to keep hidden had come with the years.

2

As HE topped the last sage hill, Snake Bend lay far below him in a pool of heat. He stopped his horse, a white-stockinged roan he had bought in Winnemucca after he'd left the train, and let his black eyes narrow in thoughtful survey. Tall and solid, he sat the saddle lazily, the brown planes of his face immobile. He wore a dark hat and suit, the legs of his pants tucked into good boots. A gun rode each hip. The pony carrying his gear caught up and stopped, its ears twitching.

In a single sweep he could discern the structure and guess the nature of the blight down there on the desert. Somewhere east in the heat-blued distance he knew Snake River slithered down from the flint-rock wastes to dart into the maw of its great stricture — Hell's Canyon. Above the canyon an ancient ford brought together all the trails and rough gumbo roads of the Oregon wasteland and western Idaho.

A spot for a helltown, and it was there — Snake Bend

whose weatherworn buildings he could see vaguely in the
glare of heat and light, the gray, huddled tents of the construction camp to the right, the strung-out rawness of new
buildings stretching away to the left. He could make out
the scratched line of the railroad grade coming out of the
south and running on north.

Even now he saw some of the traffic the Oregon Short
Line was soon to replace. Off in the east a wagon train
tooled in from railhead at Shoshone. A six-in-hand stage
came down the grade in the other direction, rolling up a
twist of dust. The line was building west from Ogden, east
from Umatilla, and the railheads were as yet three hundred
miles apart. The link-up was not expected until in the fall,
and this was a scorching August day.

Later, as he rode onto Snake Bend's main thoroughfare,
Price's first impression was resolved into a more graphic
detail. The nucleus of the town was old, weather-worn and
was skirted by several back streets, confirming his under-
standing that there had been a cowtown and freighting
station here for many years. The boom construction ran
north from it along the business street, while to the south
were the shacks and tents of the camp followers who never
failed to appear. The railroad camp was a half mile on
beyond, but between it and the town was a project that
riveted Price's interest immediately.

Men were still at work there, building a strung-out tangle
of loading pens. On this side, and against the street, was
a new frame building not yet touched by paint. Its sign
was big enough to see at a distance: SHIPSTEAD CATTLE
COMPANY.

Price turned his horse through the dust, heading that
way. The sun came bright on his left shoulder, drenching

the sage plateaus and scrub-covered, low hills. A Chinaman
padded slowly toward him. Two oil tins, hung from a
yoke, splattered river water on the dust of the street. Price
swung down at the hitchrack in front of the stockyard
office. He tied his horses and walked in, catching the smell
of new lumber and the raw reek of creosote.

A bored bookkeeper sat on a high stool over accounts
that as yet could not reflect much business. Beyond him
was the open door of an inner office. Price could see a
pair of long, booted legs and the end of a desk on past
those extremities.

The bookkeeper started to slide off the stool, but Price
said, "That Shipstead in there?"

"Yeah, but —"

"Tell him Price's here."

"Oh — they're waitin'. Go on in."

The name must have carried through the doorway. Before Price reached it, a man who did not belong to the
long legs appeared there. He was of medium height, but
a marked blockiness gave him the look of size; his middle-
aged face was sun-browned, and his hair matched its color.
The man wore a business suit, with the pants tucked into
riding boots better than Price's. He smiled and held out
his hand.

"On the dot, Price." he said heartily. "To the day and
almost to the hour. I'm Shipstead. Jim Gantry just got
here, himself."

Surveying Bent Shipstead in his quick, keen way, Price
could gain no inkling as to why Hester Carson should so
loathe and fear him. His eyes were steady, intelligent and
unafraid. But there were different kinds of steadiness, in-
telligence and courage, and this man was not easy to read.

The man with the long legs was not much older than
Price, maybe just over the thirty mark. He was tall and
lean, and there was a ball-pointed star on his vest. He
would be the county sheriff, down from Baker City for
this meeting, Price knew. Shipstead had written quite a
long letter.

Gantry rose at Shipstead's introduction and shook hands.
He took a good look at the man on the other end of the
handclasp, then sat down again with nothing more than
a casual, "Howdy."

Price was motioned toward another chair and took it
leisurely.

"Drink?" Shipstead said. "Cigar?"

Price shook his head.

Shipstead settled back into his own seat at the desk and
picked up the cigar he had laid down. Jim Gantry re-
crossed his legs and pulled out a sack of tobacco. He
wasn't saying anything at all, yet, of the two, Price somehow liked him the better.

"Well, Jim," Shipstead inquired, "do you want to depu-
tize him first, or do I pin on the marshal's badge?"

"Go ahead," said Gantry. "This is mainly your stunt."

Price looked at the sheriff thoughtfully, surprised by
the dryness of that remark. Shipstead's letter had explained
that he would receive a double commission, as Snake
Bend's marshal and as Gantry's deputy stationed at this
point. That was all right, as was the salary offered, but
Price still had a few questions to ask.

In his thin, clipped way he said, "Just a minute. Before
I take a job I want to find out more than I know about
Snake Bend. You told me you had a marshal killed on
duty. That's all right — a part of the job. But from what

I heard in Vale, he wasn't exactly on your side, Shipstead. How come?"

Shipstead gave him a quick, sharp glance. "You heard that in Vale? From whom?"

"I stopped a ruckus there. A couple of hardcases tried to abduct a girl. I broke it up. She was sure you sent them, hoping to force her brother out of hiding and into your hands. She made a remark about you having the old marshal killed so you could put your own man on the job."

"I'll be damned," Shipstead said, then was silent while he drew in a long, slow breath. "Well, I don't know a thing about last night, but that'd be Hester Carson. Price, I am trying to build them a shipping town, but half of that damned cattle crowd is bucking me. Will Carson led them. He killed a man, and two others saw it happen. Now they're all yelling frame-up, dirty deal, anything else that comes into their ringy heads."

"You've got cattlemen," Price drawled, "who don't want a loading point? That's queer."

Shipstead's thick shoulders made a shrug. "There've been a few nesters come in. The cowmen claim the railroad will bring more, and that I'm more interested in them than in the cattle trade. A heavily populated farming community would mean more business for this town, they say."

"So you're not interested in catching Will Carson?"

"I'm interested, but for the reason Gantry is. Will murdered a man. He's got to be brought to justice. But neither of us would try to use Hester to pull Will out of cover. That satisfy you?"

"No," Price said. "How about the dead marshal?"

"He was killed by some damned saddle bum he tried to disarm. The man got away. And I certainly didn't hire him to do it, although it's true that Fred Clements — that was the marshal — was a lot less interested in law and order here than I am. We had a pretty rough election a few months back. I was chosen mayor by a slim majority and by the new element that barely outnumbers the old. The Old Towners backed Clements to the hilt because he was easy on them. I thought the situation was too ticklish to fire him. His deputy, who's now acting marshal, is also an Old Town man. It's up to you whether you replace or keep him on."

"If I take the job," Price said.

"You still haven't made up your mind? When you showed up instead of writing, I took it for granted —"

"I'm interested," Price said. "But still too ignorant of the facts to suit me. Gantry, what's your problem down at this end of the county?"

Gantry glanced shrewdly at Price, who had a feeling he would like to have the man do a little of the talking.

"You named the main one," Gantry said. "My county's too damned big, and the railroad started a boom on the hind end of it."

"You've been a cowman, haven't you?"

"Most of my life."

"And you don't want a loading point here, either?"

"At present," said Gantry, "I ain't runnin' cattle. But I'm as responsible for this stinkhole as his honor here is. Snake Bend always was a tough town. It's on the freight road between the railroad in Utah and the Columbia River towns. And all the cattle drives come past here, headin' for Wyoming and Montana. We still got that, with a construction outfit, camp followers and boomers thrown in. There's as much killin' as any other crime, which happens to be county business."

Price was not unaware that Gantry had not divulged his opinion of Shipstead's plans for the town. The feeling that the sheriff did not like the mayor remained.

"Which is exactly why I want a heavy-handed marshal," Shipstead was saying. "The kind of man who tamed Bodie. Does that answer you, Price?"

"There's one thing more. If I take the job, I'll figure things out for myself and handle them my way. I won't give a damn whose toes I step on. I don't think I want your old deputy, but when I replace him, I'll pick the man. I don't patrol a street with a nightstick. If you've got a fire-arms ordinance, repeal it. That tempts more show-off gunslingers than it discourages. I never kill a man if I can get away with buffaloing him. But when I have to, I kill. I want your justice of peace and coroner to understand that beforehand."

"Agreed," Shipstead said. "But these Old Towners —"

"I don't take sides," Price interrupted. "You hire me to tame this town and I'll tame it. If that brings me up against you, then I quit being city marshal and start being deputy sheriff."

For the first time Jim Gantry grinned.

"If that suits you," Price went on slowly, "you can both swear me in."

"You're first, your honor," Gantry said lazily.

It was done quickly. Price slid both of the badges he received into his pocket. They were only tokens, and the only power that would work in this town was in his guns.

"Want to meet Judge Kerry and Doc Spears, the coroner?" Shipstead asked. "The judge is justice and police judge both. Spears also practices medicine."

"When I need 'em. What's the name of that deputy, and where does he hang out?"

"Supposed to be at the jail," Shipstead answered. "But you're more likely to find him in the Shorthorn saloon on First. I ought to warn you he thinks he should have got your job, and the Old Towners think likewise. His name's Ollie Kinkaid."

"He's a boozer?"

"On that side."

"I'll see him," Price said. "Gantry, when'll I see you again?"

"I don't figure on startin' back till tomorrow. It's a long, hard ride."

The main street, Price found as he rode back toward Old Town, was called Utah, probably for the freight road that ran to the Mormon towns. He discovered that there were four blocks to Old Town, the easternmost of the two paralleling Utah being Idaho, the one on the west Oregon. The two cross-streets were called First and Second. He was already memorizing the business establishments, as well, as he rode along idly. It was essential that he have an exact picture of the town's physical layout.

Utah Street was at least four times as long as any of the others. The new construction, running for some distance north, made a section larger than Old Town, though more strung out. Southward, in motley disarray, huddled the tent-and-shack structures of the camp followers, the hell-on-wheels gentry who moved with the construction work.

It was all here, every facet of the cyclonic centers called frontier boomtowns. He had seen them in Bodie, Hays, Trail City and in that far-off town that had taken the life of the only woman he had ever loved. Snake Bend had engendered in him already the low, ready emotion that exploded when the chips went down, that had driven and obsessed him for nearly ten years.

He found the Shorthorn just around the corner on First, across from a low plank building that obviously was the town jail. He stepped down at the saloon's hitchrack and tied his horses. Ducking under the rail, he crossed the board walk and went in through the swinging doors.

Even though he had never seen this particular saloon before, he knew at a glance that it was a trouble spot. The bullet holes in the walls and ceiling meant little; they showed in the best of places. The card tables were all out front, along the side, and even at this hour they were full. Tinhorns, he thought, not a real high roller in the bunch. At a couple of other tables men sat drinking alone, their backs to the wall. These were the careful men — men in many respects like himself, but given to violence for varying private reasons. He saw a faro layout at the back but it was not operating.

There were three men in a group at the far end of the bar, and one of them wore a badge. He had no holster, but Price saw at once the gun shoved under the band of his pants. He was middle-aged, red-faced, slope-shouldered, and his eyes were bright with drink. Price walked up to him.

For a moment he stood with his head cocked slightly as he studied Ollie Kinkaid.

"I'm Price, the new marshal," he said curtly. "I want the jail keys."

The bartender looked up in hard, quick interest. Kinkaid's eyes narrowed, and he put down the glass he held.

He had to cant his stare upward to meet Price's eyes.

"I dunno nothin' about a new marshal," he said thickly.

Patiently, Price pulled the badge from his pocket and showed it. Kincaid looked up again at Price's face.

"Where'd you buy that, sonny?" he drawled.

He wasn't prepared for what happened. Price's hand caught his shirt front and slammed him back against the bar, so hard that his head rocked heavily. Then Price yanked him forward, and Kincaid's hat fell off.

"The keys," Price said.

Kincaid started to go for the gun within tempting reach of his hand, but something in the eyes he watched changed his mind. The hand went into his pocket, instead, and came out with a ring of keys. Price took the keys, started to move off, then turned back.

"Better go tell the mayor you want your time," he said to Kincaid. "You're through."

He turned his back to the man and walked out.

He put up his horses at the Sundown Corral, knowing that the news of Snake Bend's new marshal would go through the town like flame and engender as much heat. He was bound to be challenged before many hours had passed, and felt his temper rising to the knowledge. If he could he would strike the first blow himself.

He entered the jail, found its three cells empty, and left his luggage in the small front office for the time being, to go out to get his noon meal.

In a restaurant on Utah that called itself the Golden Pheasant, he ordered a steak, hash browns, coffee and pie, and considered the human herd that he would have to

handle. First were the construction hands, probably three
thousand of them, swarming over the grades within reach
of Snake Bend on paydays. He had had experience with
them in Colorado City when the railroad came through,
knew all too well the violence of which they were capable
when they went on the loose. A criminal element always
sifted in with them, men on the dodge or on the make and
using the construction outfits for their own purposes. These
could be doubly dangerous to him since among them there
could well be someone bearing him a grudge out of the past.

Yet the gentry that made a living from this group was
worse, the breed that infested the shanties on the south
end of town — vendors of rotgut whiskey and sordid sex,
pimps, tinhorns, conmen, rollers, dopers, footpads. Add to
that the punchers from the road herds and encircling
ranges, the freighters, glory-hunters and itinerant roughs
and you had a yeasty brew. Add to it, too, the hostility
already against him in Old Town — from the men who
had supported the former marshal and Kincaid.

Yet there was a way to handle them all, by being a little
tougher than the worst of them. That must be his first step
— to establish beyond dispute that he was as rough as the
next man.

He was coming out of the restaurant when he saw the two
men he had met last night in Vale. Though he had only
seen them in the dark, their movements and such physical
features as he had detected were indelibly etched on his
trained senses. One of the two wore a bandage on his gun
hand. They were coming toward him and he paused with
a half-smoked cigarette in his fingers, which he flipped in
front of them as they came abreast.

The man named Montana stopped and hauled around

with a hard stare. "Careful where you pitch your butts, you damned dude," he said.

Price said quietly, "I hit where I aim — you two should have found that out last night in Vale."

Montana's face showed a sudden stiffening, along with recognition. He was silent for a moment, making up his mind. Finally he said with some difficulty, "All right, mister — we don't want any trouble."

"You'll get it, both of you, if you're in town come sundown."

"Now look here —" the man with the bandaged hand began, but Montana shot him a look that shut him up. They walked on without comment.

Price stared after them. If they worked for Shipstead, as Hester Carson suspected and Shipstead denied, they would not be likely to brace the marshal Shipstead had just hired, even if they cared to face his guns again. Yet they had given him his chance to assert his authority, to make his own challenge, and what they did now might tell him something.

He was turning to climb the steps of the Empress Hotel, where he meant to take a room, when he saw Jim Gantry seated in a round-backed chair on the porch. He realized from the sheriff's expression that he had seen the incident with Montana and understood its import.

"Come set a minute, Price," the sheriff called. "You can watch your town from here."

Price crossed the unpainted porch and took the chair beside Gantry. The lawman fished out tobacco and began to twist together the ingredients of a cigarette. Finally he said, "You know how to begin, Price. You're going to set this town on its ear."

"What I want from you," Price said, "is what Shipstead didn't tell me."

"Thought you never took sides."

"But I listen to 'em."

Gantry grinned. "What do you want to know?"

"How will he profit from this town if he gets it running his way instead of the Old Towners'?"

"He's building stockyards. Gonna buy cattle."

"Which has made the cowmen and Old Towners mad as hell? That's funny."

"Well," said Gantry, "the more the town booms the better for Shipstead. Him and his cronies happen to own the townsite."

For an instant Price held his breath. "When there was already a town here? How come?"

"They took up all the land they could get around it under the Townsite Act. That's three hundred and twenty acres they bought for a song and have already begun to sell high. The bigger the town is the more they can ask. The cowmen are smart enough to know that nesters can eat and use more goods than they can. That if Snake Bend is to be really big it's got to have a farm community in it."

"Then why the stockyards?"

"A gesture to the cowmen and a handful of sand in their eyes."

"These are facts?" Price asked.

"That he's building stockyards and owns a big piece of the townsite are facts. The rest is opinion."

"Then all I know," Price said, "is that he's building stockyards, owns a piece of the townsite, and wants a tame town, which I'm here to deliver. But I could use another opinion, yours, on the Carson angle."

"I can render it," said Gantry, "by telling you there used to be three men in that tough team you just tried to buffalo. Montana and Bronco Jack. Will killed one, and them two are the ones who swear it was plain murder."

"No wonder they threw a scare into Miss Carson."

"You're damned right. But you and I can only guess, as she did, that they tried to nail her to please Shipstead, and for more reasons than simple justice. Will's a leader among the cowmen and snorted the loudest about what Shipstead's tryin' to do to this cow country. On the loose, Will's a martyr and still active, you can bet. In the pen he wouldn't have much influence — and he'll have less if they can get him hung."

"As your deputy," Price asked, "am I supposed to try and catch him?"

"There's a warrant against him."

"The cattle outfits around here are probably hiding him. You must know that."

Gantry grinned. "I asked 'em, and they said they weren't. But you can ask if you want to."

"He could be guilty as charged."

"If so, you just told the star witness to hightail."

Gantry seemed to have said all he wanted on that subject and began to speak of other matters. Price would find warrants and dodgers at the jail to guide him in his conduct of the county's business. Prisoners were not to be held here but transferred to Baker City as soon as possible. The telegraph would bring somebody from down there when needed.

In conclusion, Gantry waved a hand toward the new part of the town and said, "The old-timers around here call that Shippyville. Shipstead's pardners in the townsite have all got businesses there. But believe you me they only constitute a slight majority among the permanent residents of Snake Bend."

"What do they call the hell-on-wheels on the other end of the street?"

"Cat Town. What else? They're transients and don't vote but they want things wide open."

"There's just one thing puzzles me," Price reflected. "Why didn't Shipstead pick a place for his town where he wouldn't have to buck so many natives?"

"Where else could he find a railroad that crosses a junction of the main roads in these parts? This spot has got the makings, all right. The only question is who'll run it, cattlemen or farmers?"

Price took a room, meaning to stay at the Empress only long enough to find permanent quarters. He got his luggage from the jail and took it up there, then peeled off his coat. He removed the gunbelt and slipped the sixes into his leather-lined hip pockets again. That was a trick he had learned from Dallas Stoudenmire, the most comfortable, unobtrusive way to carry hardware, yet assure a quick draw. He washed the trail dust off his face.

He spent the rest of the afternoon completing his inspection of Snake Bend. There were no saloons or obvious sex stores in Shippyville, which didn't look much like it meant to cater to a cattle trade. There were many new buildings going up, and he saw dwellings on unimproved back streets.

Old Town still caught his main interest. There were four big mercantiles on Utah, and more saloons than he bothered to count. There was a place calling itself the Gillette Variety Theater and a few other doors to indicate that there had long been sex service here. Down in Cat Town there was a huge tent that doubtless was a dance hall. These places he noticed, among a far greater number of more sedate establishments, for they were the springs of violence.

He ate his supper at the Snake Cafe. When he came out the sun was westering upon the gray hills toward the great desert. Neither Montana nor his saddlemate, Bronco Jack, were in sight.

He stepped into the Great Western for the first of the two drinks he allowed himself each day, and he made it brandy as usual. This was a place that policed itself, he knew immediately. Physically, it differed from others in no wise except the high quality of its decor and the relative sedateness of its atmosphere. It would draw the independent cowmen, the bigwigs among the railroad men, and the upper crust of the town. Its game room was mostly concealed beyond a wide arch in the back wall, and as he looked that way Price's black eyes showed an abrupt interest.

A man, patently a gambler, came through the arch. He was elegantly dressed, wearing striped trousers, a black frock coat and a silk tile hat. A magnificent mustache flowed out from his rotund, handsome face, and there was a genial courtesy in the way he came through the crowd. When he saw Price, he let his mouth crease even more pleasantly, and came over.

"Hell, Sam," Price said. "So this is where you came when you left Bodie."

Sam Wens offered his hand and his grip was firm. "But you didn't surprise me," he murmured. "I've been hearing nothing but Mason Price all afternoon. Have one on me."

"You know one at a time's my limit, Sam."

"For which I'd hold you in vast contempt," said Wens,

"except I know that when you get in a game there's no limit."

Price grinned. Sam Wens was a high-roller, one of the best and straightest gamblers in the West. Once he had gone into a Bodie bank and borrowed ten thousand on a promissory note, with the banker knowing he was taking it into a game. Price was glad to see him, for by now Wens would know this town inside and out. Although he would not inform on anyone, whatever his contempt for the scum of his profession, he had dropped more than one hint that had saved Price's life.

Now he said, "I know a man a lot of other men are plying with booze — and pointing out how affronted he's been."

"The deputy I fired?"

"Did you fire a deputy?" Sam Wens seemed surprised. "You son of a gun!" He gave Price's shoulder a slap and went on.

Price was out on the street as the shadows lengthened. He walked to the north end of Utah on the east side, crossed over and came back on the other. He made his first circuit through Cat Town, quiet now, dead and deserted — it was both early and between railroad paydays. Finally he went back along Utah to the jail.

Montana and Bronco Jack were not on the street, and he wasn't going to search the hundred possible places where they could be loitering in defiance of his orders. They knew they could not show themselves in this town again without trouble as long as he was there. Therefore, his cold mind calculated precisely, they would either have left or would look him up to try their luck at removing him.

He smoked a cigarette in the jail office, his feet up on

the old desk. There was a calculated reason for his dis-
continuing his rounds for the night. A man fell too easily
into grooved routines that could set him up for future
trouble. Moreover, there was a psychological advantage
in his insolent assurance that his presence in a town was
enough to hold it in check.

Besides the desk and swivel chair, the office held an old
filing cabinet whose contents Price meant to examine some
dull day. Next to it was a gun rack that held a rifle and a
shotgun, which he examined and found to be in good shape.
A gaboon and a fly swatter completed the furnishings.

Around ten he went out again. Pianos and three-piece
bands had struck up all over town. There were some fifty
cow ponies strung along the racks of Old Town, punchers
from the near ranches or perhaps from passing road herds
on their way east. Twice that many construction hands
had come over from the camp. The tent dancehall in Cat
Town had opened for business but its trade was small and
orderly. Price went down a sidestreet to the cribs, to acquaint
himself with their layout.

Tonight his reputation was doing most of his work for
him. The town would keep a rein on itself until it knew
just how far it could go. He went back through Old Town
on Idaho, passing a dignified dwelling with three cow
ponies with different brands in front. He didn't need to be
told it was a parlor house.

He came back to First and stepped into the Shorthorn,
where he had taken the jail keys from Ollie Kincaid. The
man was there, sharing a table with three others who
seemed to be engaging him in earnest conversation. The
talk broke off when they saw Price, but none of them
showed open hostility. Price wondered suddenly if he had

mistaken Sam Wens' meaning. Maybe the gambler had
meant that Montana was getting liquored in some deadfall
and was being pushed to call for a showdown. That made
sense, for Kincaid looked drunk enough to fall over.

The faro layout was working now, a man in a derby
dealing, while a stocky, pockmarked individual was keeping
case. There was a lookout chair, but it was empty. Price's
jaded glance shifted to a runty youngster who was bucking
the game. There were three or four others, either playing
or watching. The man next to the short puncher was
shabby, dirty, and Price noted that he had his holster tied
down. A typical tough hombre.

Price was about to turn away when the youngster
whirled on the rough. He said, "Mister, keep your hand
off my bet." The hardcase swung around, bristling, and
Price stood ready to step in.

"Take it easy, gents!" the dealer said uneasily. "Whose
bet is it?"

"Mine," the hardcase growled.

"You're a damned liar, mister."

The older man cursed and his hand stabbed for his gun.
Before he had cleared leather, and before Price could
intercede, a gun had whipped up into the frail youngster's
hand, its muzzle under the rough's chin.

"Clear out, you dirty son," the puncher said calmly,
"or I'll blow the top off your head."

The rough swung and made for the door. The puncher
shoved his gun back into holster and returned his attention to the game. He picked up the bet he had won, grinned
at the dealer, then made his way to the bar.

Price was cautious about coming up on him, but the
puncher glanced at the marshal, an easy, friendly grin on

his face. His hair was sandy, and his pinched features reflected a lot of living in the outdoors. Price's decision was
made.

"I'm the new marshal here," he said, "and I hope that
was really your bet."

"It was. The dealer knew it but was scared of that big
bugger."

"What's your name?"

"Shorty Harris."

"Where you from?"

Harris took a moment about answering that. "Here and
there."

"Good enough. Where you heading?"

"West. Lookin' for a ridin' job."

"I fired a deputy today. You want a job like that?"

Harris looked interested. "What's it pay?"

"Seventy-five, and you can sleep in the jail." That was
double riding pay.

"You're that Price hombre from Bodie, ain't you?"
Harris asked. "I been hearing the talk around here."

"I'm Price. How about it, Shorty? You want to give
me a chance to get a little sleep now and then?"

"Mister, you can go to bed right now."

"You can start tomorrow. Come see me at the jail."

Harris grinned. "You better know it, Marshal — it'll be
the first time I was ever anxious to do that. But I'll be
there."

Price was pleased with his luck as he went out. Harris'
history was of no interest to him as long as the fellow
possessed the speed and the nerve he had shown.

At eleven Price had a cup of coffee in a Shippyville
restaurant that still smelled of new paint. This part of town

gave no evidence of night life. Shipstead was enforcing decorum for the expected farm family trade. Yet for all its graveyard quiet, the section came close to costing Price his life.

He was passing some new construction when the warning came, the inner awareness of danger that had moved him into action the night before in Vale. He felt it as he came abreast the half-finished building and instantly stopped on a forward stride and threw himself back just as a streak of fire and a blasting roar rent the night. A shotgun.

Rage boiled in him, and as the second barrel gushed its load, both of Price's guns were out. He smashed four shots into the precise spot of the blasts before the shotgun echoes died. A handgun answered him from a point some ten feet to the right. Two more bullets from Price's guns slashed through the night. He saw a man stagger forward from behind a post and go down. There was no more shooting.

The street came alive farther down. Price stood warily, anger seething and turning in him. Then he moved forward to investigate. He expected to find Montana and Bronco Jack, but the man face down across the shotgun didn't look like either one. The other man also, his chest cut open by bullets, was a total stranger. Sure that neither would give him more trouble, Price went back to the first and rolled him over.

It was Ollie Kincaid.

The poor damned fool, Price thought. Too drunk to cut it, even with a shotgun, yet he tried. Price wondered why. It couldn't be pride alone, or even pride combined with whiskey. Somebody had made a tool of Kincaid — perhaps the man who had helped the ex-deputy pay the price.

Price stepped out to the walk.

Boots pounded on the boards. Men moved past him. "I'm a egg-suckin' hound," somebody bawled, "if it wasn't a shotgun trap! Dammit, what bottle ever held enough to give Ollie the nerve?"

Shorty Harris came out of the shadows and stopped beside Price. Quietly, he said, "Marshal, I can take care of this town the rest of the night, and you need a drink. Go and get it."

Price stared at him. This was the one man in Snake Bend from whom there was no need to hide his feelings. Harris knew. Price nodded.

"Have somebody take the bodies to the coroner," he said. That's Doc Spears." He headed down the street, and the walk under him seemed a little uneven.

3

GILLETTE'S Variety Theater was all but emptied when Price stepped in, yet word of the shooting was there ahead of him. He caught the faint hostility already in the room and at once multiplied it by the number of other establishments in Old Town. Kincaid had been their man. The new marshal had killed him. The indisputable evidence of ambush would be discounted, the feeling implemented that the marshal was a Shipstead hireling.

The place was like many others of its kind — there was a stage across the deep end of the room, tables and chairs filling the rest of the floor, while a horseshoe balcony of

curtained boxes ran along the front and sides. Price ordered
a double brandy, took it and turned toward the stairs.

At the top he stepped into the nearest box, left the curtain undrawn and took seat at the small table with a wall
to his back. He put down the drink and lighted a cigarette.
Tiredly, he listened. The floor below began to fill up again.
Men passed, moving to the other boxes to drink and watch
the show that was about due.

The hungers in him were fullest when he had narrowly
escaped death. He had often marked the fact, both in himself and others, that the lusts of life ran strongest when
life had been at stake. His experience of the past ten years
had conditioned in him three strong appetites, two of
which he had always to deny. One was for violence, and
this he never let progress, for when a man started hunting
it he became less than a man. The next was for drink, and
these were the only times he felt a desire to go on a real
bender. There were gunfighters who indulged that impulse
and through it came invariably to grief.

Finally there was want of a woman, and this was strong
in him now. With the proper safeguards, he could indulge
it, and he had come here to look around. The hookers in
the cribs were pure poison for a man in his trade, the
parlor houses not much better. But with an entertainer in
a place like this a man could sometimes make arrangements
that were satisfactory.

He sipped his brandy and smoked until he grew aware
of piano music on the floor below. The buzz of voices lowered, the lazy music took on energy. He drew the curtain
and watched a team come out on the little stage to do its
song and dance — a man in a derby and checked suit, a
pert, black-haired girl with bare legs, a short skirt and

tight upper garment. A placard on the side of the stage
said "The High Steppers." The song was mediocre, but the
dance that followed was brisk, expert and pulled down the
house. Beaming, the team bowed out, and a shuffling clown
juggler came on. Price lost interest.

His nerves had started to loosen, and he realized that
the killing of Kincaid could bring a crisis to the town. The
men who had crowded the fool into it might have wanted
just that. He was glad he found Harris, a stranger without
side . . .

He saw her going past the open curtain, the little dancer,
and his suspicion was confirmed that she was a box rustler,
too. Maybe she was going to someone else, but when their
eyes met he smiled and she stopped.

"How about a drink with me?" he asked.

She smiled and nodded, but went on toward the stairs,
still wearing the provocative little skirt but with a shawl
about her shoulders now. She was small and slender, and
he could feel the lifting beat of his heart. She was back
presently, slipping into the seat across the table, again
smiling at him.

"You're the new marshal, aren't you?" she said. "Somebody pointed you out to me today."

"I'm Price. What's your name?"

"Trixie. Maybe I oughtn't to pull it on the marshal, but
I ordered a bottle of wine."

"I'll buy it, but I didn't come here to drink. Was the
fellow you danced with your mac?"

She shook her head. "I don't have a mac."

"Then that leads to another question."

"I know. Do I put out. I don't."

"Why not?"

A smile formed on the girl's mouth. "I make more from
their wanting it than I would if I delivered."

"Not from me you won't, Trixie."

She regarded him thoughtfully. "Is this a squeeze, Marshal?"

"No," Price said. "Just a man wheedling a girl who
looks mighty good to him."

"Thanks. Here comes the wine."

A waiter brought the bottle on a tray with two glasses.
Price paid for it, knowing that while he might put himself under the table Trixie wouldn't down one good drink
all night. He filled a glass for her but continued his slow
sipping of the brandy. He lighted fresh cigarettes and
gave one to her. He thought he had got behind her front,
that she was considering his proposition. She was a pretty
little thing, with a warmth in her eyes that could be reward-
ing to the right man.

She said, "What's your first name?"

"Mason. Mace for short."

"Well, I like you, Mace, and I want to tell you something. There are people around here who figure you won't
last long."

"I know that. Does it ruin my chances with you?"

Trixie looked thoughtful. "If you mean my liking you,
it's just the opposite. I kind of go for a man who can
scare everybody half to death. Maybe it's cheap, but it
takes one like that to give me a thrill."

"Glad to oblige any time," Price murmured.

"Thanks. I'll remember. And I'm not going to sit here
trying to fleece a man who knows my game better than I
do." She rose, small, supple and provocative as hell to him.
At the curtain she paused, her head cocked pertly. "Hope

I didn't sound too discouraging, Marshal," she added and
vanished.

Price went down the stairs. He was aware of attracting
attention with every step he took first to the door, then to
the street. All at once he saw Snake Bend in all its bleak
ugliness and knew he had not begun to get his bite into
the town. The reason was plain enough. The conflict was
not only the lawless pitted against those who preferred
decency and order. There was a political division, with the
new mayor on one side and the town that had been here
before him on the other.

The cattlemen backing Old Town seemed convinced that
they were fighting to protect their range from the nesters
Shipstead might try to attract to the country. Price wished
he had a means of getting their side of it more clearly, of
exerting some degree of steadying influence on them. That
seemed to be the only way he could drain the deep lesion
poisoning Snake Bend.

The coroner's jury delivered its verdict around ten
o'clock, the next morning — justifiable homicide. While
he had been uneasy, Price was not greatly surprised. In
the light of day the evidence of the ambush could not be
argued.

Afterwards he went to see Shipstead and had the name
of Shorty Harris entered on the town payroll. While the
mayor did not seem too pleased with the wispy stranger,
he was enormously so with Price's first day in Snake Bend.

"That's what it takes," he said, "and you've got my
backing right down the line."

"That's not all it takes." Price stared across the wide desk
in Shipstead's office at the stockyards. "What's needed is
some demonstration on your part that you don't intend to

fill this country with dirt farmers. What makes your opposition so damned sure?"

"Cussedness," Shipstead said readily. "Will Carson was a trail driver. He handled a lot of cattle that wasn't his own. When the railroad knocks out the trail drives he's going to be out of a job. So he keeps working on the ranchers, and they're mossyhorns enough about change to fall in with him."

"You're saying they're against shipping by rail. I doubt that like hell. It's you they distrust. Why?"

"If you find out," Shipstead said calmly, "let me know. I keep wondering, myself."

"I intend to find out," Price assured him.

Leaving Harris on duty, he got his horse from the livery and rode west on the Vale road. The sun came on his left shoulder and painted his foreshortened shadow on the sandy soil. Ahead, he saw fold upon fold of the dry sage hills. This was big scenery, to the farthest of horizons. It was one big cow pasture that, without irrigation, could never be anything else.

Vale prickled out of the landscape before him and he rode in, going at once to the hat store where he hoped to find Hester Carson. He racked his horse in front and walked stolidly in to find her alone and astonished. She wore a fresh, neat dress, and her hair was smoothly combed now, but there sprang into her eyes the hostility he had seen there the other night.

"Doesn't Shipstead ever give up?" she asked.

Price removed his hat and stood holding it, meeting the unwavering stare of her eyes. "You ought to back off and take another run at it, Miss Carson. You jumped to the wrong conclusion about me."

She dismissed that with an impatient motion of the hand.
"Why are you here?"

"I'd like to get in touch with your brother."

Hester threw back her head and laughed. "So would
every other Shipstead man. Will you tell me you're not on
the Shipstead payroll?"

"No. But I think you'll tell him about me. When you do
I wish you'd tell him it might help him and me both if we
got together on the quiet."

"Help you how?"

"I hired out to tame Snake Bend, and I'll tame it. From
what I've learned, I think the trouble between Shipstead
and the cowmen has got to be settled before the place will
ever simmer down. I've heard Shipstead's side. I'd like to
hear Will's — unless you think another man would put
it better."

"What you'd like," she retorted, "is to see Will hung."

"If he's guilty, that'd be my duty. I don't know whether
he is or isn't, and right now I don't care. You're set on
calling me a Shipstead man, but Gantry's made me his
deputy as well. You must know he leans to the cowmen's
side. Why'd he want me if he thought like you do, that I've
sold my guns to his honor the mayor?"

He grinned, and watched the effect on her. Her face
tilted up, her cheeks showing increased temper. "I can
tell you one thing," she breathed. "I'm too smart for you
to use to trap Will."

"Just tell him what I said and see what he thinks."

He turned and walked out.

He was back in Snake Bend for his noon meal. The
streets were quiet, and Harris was napping on a chair at
the jail. Price didn't disturb him. Stepping back onto the

sun-seared walk, he gave thought to finding himself living quarters that would be safer and more to his liking than his room in the hotel.

He thought of Sam Wens and made his way to the Great Western. The gambler was there, engrossed in a newspaper just in by the stage from Umatilla. Price seated himself at the table Wens had preëmpted, keeping his back to the wall. Wens folded the paper and shoved it into his coat pocket.

"You earned your first day's wages," he said.

Price shrugged. "I killed two men — neither the man I thought I was shooting at. And maybe raised billy hell with the prospects of keeping this town in line."

The gambler nodded thoughtfully. "You sure did, but I wouldn't gamble on everybody wanting you dead just because of that."

"Sam, I want a room where I won't have to sleep with one eye open every night. You know of anything?"

A smile twisted the ends of Sam Wens' mouth. "I was about to make a suggestion along that line. It happens I'm renting the upstairs of Doc Spear's little building. Outside stairs and two nice big rooms. One I haven't used. I'd like to rent it, to keep from getting a neighbor I don't like. The coroner's office is downstairs, but that makes medical assistance real handy — if you don't mind sleeping above a corpse almost every night."

"What's around it?"

"The stairs go up from an alley, but there's only one door for you to worry about and it's got a chain on it. Window's visible from Utah, a lighted street. I was thinking that we might make good watchdogs for each other."

"Fine. I'll take it."

"Without seeing it?" Wens inquired. "Marshal, don't ever trust a gambler."

Price said softly, "You were the one said I'd bet to the limit."

Wens shook his head, fished a key from his pocket and handed it over. "Door on the left as you go up. The privy is private and no less fragrant than the others in Snake Bend."

Price took a look at the room, liked it and moved in. Stairs led up to it from an unobtrusive alley. The door at the top landing could be double-locked, and only two doors opened from the hallway beyond. Sam Wens ran many risks, himself, and had chosen the place with care.

Later he stretched out on the bed and found it soft and comfortable. There was a cold stove in one corner to stand against the winter that would soon howl over the desert. He let the tensions drain out of him and nearly fell asleep.

Rising finally, he went out and had a cup of coffee in the Little Gem, then walked over to the jail.

Harris was awake and yawning noisily. He said, "Howdy, Marshal. Kinda went to sleep at the switch, didn't I?"

"Considering that you were up all night, I think that's just fine. Better set up your cot and get some real sleep. Want you handy from about ten tonight on."

"Slept enough for now."

"How long have you been around, Shorty?"

"Couple of days. Long enough to go broke."

"And learn something about this town," Price added. "Well, the railroad has a payday Saturday. Two days from now. If you were going to run a few characters out of town before then, to keep things quieter, who'd you run?"

"Two-three tinhorns I know of, and a few hookers. That faro game in The Bank is crooked. Man called The Bishop deals, and his case man and lookout are gunnies from way back. There's a dance hall in Cat Town with some real bitches. Or is there any such thing as a bitch cat? They call the place the Big Tent."

"I'll take care of it," Price said. "What did you think of Shipstead?"

"The man's crooked as a dog's hind leg."

"That's right, and we might have to take him on before we get this town gentled."

"Wouldn't he tie a can to us?" Harris asked.

"I'm a deputy sheriff, too. If need be, I can get you made one. The county's got as much reason as Shipstead, and maybe a more honest one, for wanting this place salted down."

Price went first to the owner of the Big Tent, an ex-gandy-dancer named O'Toole. He said, "You've got a few girls here with the earmarks of she-wolves. Here're their names. Get rid of them before sundown, Friday night." He dropped a slip of paper on the man's desk.

O'Toole stared at it, then scowled up at Price. "Now, you look here!" he spluttered. "I'm runnin' this place."

"I said get rid of them."

4

HE WENT from the Big Tent to The Bank, knowing that the gambling den presented an entirely different problem. Women made trouble of one kind in a wide-open town—the

crooked gamblers were an even uglier breed, far more independent and dangerous. Price, as he entered, saw that
the faro layout was not working but he recognized the
tinhorn who owned it.

The Bishop was a stately man, tall, gray, and dressed in
flawless black. There was a bulge on the left side of his
chest, and his hands, as he regarded the marshal, looked
nervous. He possessed little of the affability of Sam Wens
and not a trace of Wens' honesty.

"I hear Saturday's payday," Price told him.

The tinhorn stared at him. "Now, isn't that remarkable?
I happened to hear the same rumor."

"Heard yet that you won't be here?"

"No."

"You're hearing it now."

The Bishop's breath made a sibilant hiss as he drew it
in. "You sure I hear?" he said, his voice very soft.

"This is your chance to argue it. If you're here after
sundown Friday, you might stay permanent — under
ground."

He waited, meeting the gambler's eyes. The Bishop said
nothing, and presently Price turned and walked back outside.

The afternoon was soon marked by a merciless heat.
The desert wind died and the town's rank odors hung in
the dead air. Harris had found a cot and set it up in the
jail office and was sleeping again, but Price knew he would
be wide awake from sundown on. A huge freight outfit
pulled through town from the Columbia, on its way to
Kelton on the Union Pacific. Price heard that another eastbound road herd was on the prairie southward, which
meant more cowboys would be in town that night.

He ate supper in the Empress dining room, had his after-supper brandy in its bar, then stepped onto a street whose heat seemed not to have lessened a bit. As the shadows lengthened the first punchers hit town, riding in a noisy group, but they were soon scattered out. Shorty Harris had caught up with his rest and was on the street. Shippyville was locked up for the night except for its hotels and eating houses, but Cat Town was getting noisy.

Around ten Price met Harris on the corner of Second and Utah. The runty deputy had his hands slid into his hip pockets and his hat rode the back of his head.

As casually as if discussing the heat, Harris said, "Feelin' their oats down there," and tipped his head toward the shacktown down the street. "No accident about it, either. Time to go see what they've got fixed for us?"

"I'll go pretty soon."

"Better let me watch your backtrail, Marshal. They've got some real lowlifers down there. Man like you ought to be killed by somebody in his own class, at least."

"Come on, then. Let's see what's up."

The off-street cribs were emitting drunken laughter and racket, but the main hubbub came from the Big Tent. Price stepped in, Harris trailing him, and saw O'Toole just inside the entrance, chewing a stogie and watching the two officers. The proprietor's tight, florid face showed that he was spoiling for trouble.

The place wasn't even half-filled, Price saw, although there were a number of spurred boots scraping the floor, and a few construction hands who still seemed to have money to spend. Then he detected the source of the hilariousness. O'Toole had been letting his girls drink, a sure way to avoid a peaceable night. Except for the noise, there wasn't a thing to complain about as yet. But the place would blow up before morning, and when it did it would be for the sheer purpose of trying to eliminate the marshal.

A big, half-drunk cowpoke with a girl drunker yet, swung through the entrance. As they came around, the girl stopped, loosening herself from the puncher's hot grasp, and pointed.

"Oh, lookee!" she shrilled, "That cute little bantie with the great big badge on his shirt."

"This is it, Marshal," Harris said quietly, "and the bitch made it my move."

"Go ahead," Price whispered.

Harris sauntered out onto the floor, where the couple still stood watching. There was the faintest smile on his mouth as he stared at the woman. He said something so softly that Price couldn't hear, but it had its effect.

"Why, damn you!" the puncher bawled and reached for his gun.

Before it was half out of leather, Harris had buffaloed him, his .45 whipping upward and its barrel crashing against the side of the man's head. The puncher grunted and went down in a cold drop. Silence surged into the room, the music died clear away.

Harris had swung, his gun covering the others. "The first man that moves is dead."

They seemed to believe him for they stood still.

"This deadfall's tryin' to use you boys," Harris said, more mildly. "Get you to do their killin' for 'em. Believe that, or be shown." He backed off the floor until he came to Price, who had both hands under the tails of his coat.

Walking over to O'Toole, then, Price said, "Lock up till these women are sober. I don't intend to put you out of business, but try anything like this again and I sure will."

O'Toole's black Irish temper was seething. "The girls got hold of some booze—" he began.

"Sure. Lock up, O'Toole. And if that woman's name isn't on the list I gave you, put it on. That and keeping order here is all I'm asking of you."

"All right," O'Toole said on a long, low breath. "I'll close for the night. But I ain't so sure they'll leave town. They don't only work here. Some of 'em have got their own pimps, an' they might not see it your way."

"Told them what I said?"

"Yeah."

"Tell 'em again."

By the time Price and Harris were back on the streets of Old Town, the shack-and-tent section was strangely quiet. Not long afterward Price saw that the lights in the Big Tent had been put out. The incident seemed to have a quieting effect on the whole town. When Price went to his room at three o'clock he had had no more trouble.

Friday was another hot day. At ten o'clock, Snake Bend lay in arid drowsiness, with scarcely a man to be seen on the street. But they worked on the railroad grade, the bridges on the Snake, and around noon another big freight outfit tooled in from the Shoshone railhead. The Kelton-bound stage rattled through from Baker City, on its way to the ferry at the river. Price heard blasts farther down the grade, where a section of tough lava rock was being removed. He wondered what the situation would be when the sun sank below the bare hills toward the coast.

At three o'clock he saw four hacks pull out of the Sundown livery and swing onto Utah, heading south. From the shade of the board awning fronting Frankmeir's mer-

cantile in Old Town he watched the rigs pull up in front
of the Big Tent. He didn't move any closer, for he was
convinced that O'Toole and his soiled doves had seen the
light.

Women began to emerge from the seamy apertures of
Cat Town, a few men. They had decided that while they
might find less profit elsewhere, they would find more
security. The hacks loaded and pulled out to the south,
probably heading up the grade for Shoshone or one of the
other new towns along the line.

He stayed out of The Bank, although no hack pulled up
before its door or before those of the town's hotels. The
Kelton stage hadn't picked up a passenger, and Price knew
that when it came to The Bishop he had a real showdown
to face.

He ate his supper at six, with sundown still over two
hours away, went to the jail, where Harris said, "Well,
Marshal, they're gonna try and pull your whiskers. Was it
me, I wouldn't give 'em a chance."

"What'd you do?"

"I'd take you and me and go in there shootin' before
they expect it. That's a animal breed. The world's better
off with 'em dead and planted."

Price gave him a cool grin. "I agree with that last."

"You're goin' alone?"

"The minute the shadows stretch across Utah."

He tilted back in one of the chairs, his hat canted over
his eyes, and seemed to fall asleep. He was without feeling except for the anger that already had begun to simmer
in him, deep down.

Harris didn't have to tell him when the time had come.
Price straightened in his chair, lighted a cigarette, took a

look at his guns and slid them back into his hip pockets. He returned to Utah, crossed to the far sidewalk, and stepped past the few doors that brought him to The Bank. By then the shadows of the buildings on the west side of the street fell on the opposie walls. The walks were empty, as he expected, for word of the showdown had spread.

The saloon was nearly empty, too, but The Bishop was there, seated at a table with his two helpers in the faro layout. The other tinhorns were staying in character, taking no chances they were not forced to take, yet ready to move back and profit, should the marshal lose out.

Price paused close to the door to let his eyes adjust to the weaker light.

"Sundown," Price called to the group. "Or didn't you notice, Bishop?"

One of The Bishop's companions had his right hand below the table top, which could be a design to puzzle and confuse the marshal. The other had his arms on the table, was resting his weight on his elbows. Price could feel a muscle tic at the corner of his right eye, and his fury was rising. He was as much a killer now as any man in the room.

"Bartender," he said, "the boys down there seem to have wax in their ears. Go tell them I'm going to kill every man not on his feet, with his hands up, in just five seconds."

The saloon-keeper looked ill. "They hear you!" he bawled, then, seeming to realize he had used up some of the time, he ducked behind the bar.

The thing Price had half expected happened. The man with his arms on the table let his hand slide like a darting snake into his left coat sleeve and come out with a double-barreled derringer. Price felt his own guns buck and recoil, without realizing how they had come into his hands. The derringer exploded, then was flung upward by a jerking arm. The Bishop kicked over the table, ducking behind it with the other man. They began pouring lead blindly through the thin table top.

Price lunged to the right, holding his fire. When the guns of the other two paused, he fired once, shifted position instantly, and was answered by another salvo.

When the next halt came in the firing he called sharply, "Stand with your hands up and empty, damn you!"

The Bishop and the other forted with him lost no time in obeying. Price already knew the man who had tried to flash a hideout gun would never rise again.

"I ought to send you out in a pine box," Price said savagely, "but you might as well take some others with you. Pass the word that I'll kill any other damned tinhorn I find in this town tomorrow. Take your women with you."

The Bishop didn't look dignified, as he hustled toward the door. The other man was close on his heels.

The saloon owner climbed to his feet, his mouth open, his cheeks loose and empty. "You know how it is, Marshal!" he blurted. "They decide to move in on your place, and you can't stop 'em!"

"Don't let any more move in and we'll forget it," Price said.

He had the dead tinhorn's body picked up and taken to the coroner's. Afterwards he sat in the jail office with a grinning Harris while the town's two livery stables did a land office business. The day's shakedown had cleaned out the worst element. At two in the morning Snake Bend was completely quiet.

Price had brandy in his own room now and decided it

would be wise to go there for his nightcap. Tramping along the serene, nearly empty street he was again feeling the stir of life hungers that came after violence. They touched him with a rare loneliness, yet he climbed the stairs, entered his room and prepared for bed.

He had stripped to the waist and was sitting in the now cooler breeze from the window, sipping brandy, when he heard quick, light steps in the hallway. He sat motionless, listening, then a low voice called to him.

"Don't shoot. It's me."

He knew the voice, and a smile creased the ends of his mouth as he stepped to the door and opened it. The light fell on Trixie, who was smiling, looking like she felt as good as he did suddenly. She stepped quickly inside, and he shut and locked the door again.

"I hoped you'd come."

"I guess I knew the other night I was going to."

"Through for the night?" he said, watching her narrowed eyelids.

"I hope I'm just starting."

He crossed over and blew out the light.

5

THE RAILROAD payroll came in under guard Saturday afternoon and by evening, as the paymaster passed from camp to camp, men swarmed the streets of Snake Bend bent upon achieving poverty again as speedily as possible.

Price, after a coroner's inquest had returned a verdict of justified homicide in the case of the dead tinhorn, sensed a new feeling in the town. He was no more popular. Yet there were men who moved more freely now, pleasure-bound, a little surer of getting what they paid for.

At midnight the Big Tent was still operating quietly, O'Toole on hand and carefully keeping order, his girls sober and aware that to remain in Snake Bend they had to behave. The cribs, while busy, created no disturbance. There were only a few low-stake games at The Bank, the players all construction hands or punchers.

The faro layout was gone from the Shorthorn. The parlor house on Idaho had its blinds drawn sedately, emitted no noise. Shorty Harris broke up a rough-and-tumble between a husky freighter and an even bigger gandydancer, while Price disarmed a cowpoke who emptied his gun into the air on Utah. Then things settled down again.

Thus Price was nearly caught flat-footed when the trouble came to him. He was on the west side of Utah when something lashed out snakelike from the dark, narrow canyon between Frankmeir's store and the new empty building beside it, hurtling toward him. He leaped aside, saw a catch-rope hit the sidewalk, heard a man's quick, low curse.

In the next seconds boots were striking the ground hard enough to drum up sound. Price might have killed the man had he risked lungng into the dark alley, but he had a feeling more than one man was involved in the ambush. Moreover, he wanted to know who would try to capture rather than cut him down.

He plunged on to the corner, turned west, then ran swiftly toward Oregon. The silent attack had attracted no attention. As he came onto Oregon he saw two horses, with men scrambling urgently to leather.

"Halt or I'll fire!" Price shouted.

The horses leaped out, and his right gun roared. One of the figures threw sudden arms into the air, swayed and fell from the saddle. The other whipped his mount onto First and went thundering out toward the desert. The shot drew a shout from Utah, but by then Price was running to the unstirring figure on the ground. There was danger that the escaped rider would try to circle back through the alley and pick up his fallen companion.

He stood over the downed man menacingly in a matter of seconds, but the danger from this one was slight. After one desperate effort to push up, the man dropped flat again. He had no gun in his hand, nor had he dropped one, and Price saw that the piece still rode in the man's holster. This puzzled him enormously.

Shorty Harris came pounding up and yelled, "What you got there, Marshal?"

"Damned if I know," Price answered.

Then others were stirring about him, men dragged from bars and gaming tables by the outburst of excitement. Somebody struck a match, then a voice ripped out.

"I'll be damned! He got Will—Will Carson!"

The words pounded on Price's awareness. Carson? Why would he try so insane a thing as roping a marshal? Then the full meaning tore through Price. Here was the wanted man, helpless, in custody finally—and taken by Mason Price.

"All right," he heard himself saying. "Clear out. That's all there was to it."

"But what happened, Marshal?"

"All I know is he tried to rope me and didn't make it."

"You heard what the man said," rapped Harris. "Clear out, all of you."

Price was confronted suddenly by an urgent problem. When the gallery had dissolved, he used a match of his own to make a more careful inspection of Carson. The man was hit low in his right shoulder. The shock of the bullet and the smashing fall from his plunging horse still had him half senseless. Shot in the back. Somehow the thought of having done that sickened Price.

"What in hell were you up to, Carson?" he asked hoarsely.

Carson didn't answer, maybe didn't even hear. Price lifted him—by the book the place to take him was the jail, but this man was hurt badly. So Price took his first county prisoner to his own room over Doc Spears' office.

The coroner's windows were dark. Price said to Harris, who had followed him, "Get the medico, wherever he is."

"What's so important about this hombre?" Harris wanted to know.

"If shooting him does to this town what I think it will, you'll find out. Go on, Shorty. Then get back here. I got to send a telegram to the sheriff."

"Must be big stuff," Harris said and was gone.

Price placed Carson on the bed, then went over and lighted the lamp. Ripping away Will's shirt, he exposed the wound, which still bled profusely and was dangerously low on the chest. Going to his dresser, he got a couple of clean handkerchiefs. By tearing up a pillow slip, he managed to get a compress into place to check the flow of blood. Carson was growing restless, beginning to get hold of his faculties.

Harris came thumping up the stairs and stopped in the

doorway. "They say the doc's over in Vale. Got friends there and sometimes spends the night."

"Send somebody after him. Carson has a sister in Vale— better send word for Hester Carson to come, too. I don't know if he's got a chance."

"Sure." Harris was gone again.

Seated in a chair beside the bed, finally, Price smoked and studied his prisoner. He saw nothing that suggested a desperado, nothing but a young man with a whiskery, weathered face beginning to draw tight with pain—the kind of buckaroo, basically, you could find on a hundred cattle ranges.

Then Carson's eyes came open wildly. His jaw clenched as he tried to push himself up from the bed.

"Easy," Price said. "No use, Carson. You made a damned fool play and it backfired on you."

"So the great Price's—as good as—he's supposed to be."

"You're not the kind of lunatic that would want to find out for himself. Why'd you try to rope me?"

"Damn you," Carson breathed. "You told Hester—if we talked—it might do some good. I—didn't aim to talk— without holdin' the whip hand."

"You chucklehead," Price breathed. "Why didn't you get word to me?"

"I don't—trust you worth a damn—myself. But I did figure—it was worth talkin' to you."

A bitter frustration filled Price. Hester had done what he had asked, and now her brother was in the hands of the law, a prisoner. You couldn't blame Will for wanting to hold the upper hand when he did his talking with a man who held a warrant over him. It was too late now to turn him loose. Not only had a dozen men seen and recognized him—he was in no shape to look out for himself. So Jim Gantry had to get him for Carson's own safety.

"Think I was set for you?" he asked thinly. "That it was a trick to get you close enough to shoot?"

"What am I supposed to think? You ducked that catch-rope like you expected it."

"A man gets hunches, Carson. In my game he needs to."

"It's a damned rotten game, believe me."

"That depends on who's playing it."

Carson's strength was returning, the color creeping back into his cheeks. Thoughts were coming with them, black and desperate, and Price would have given much to know what they were.

Then somebody hammered on the door.

Price scowled and started to ignore the summons. On second thought, he walked over and opened the door. Bent Shipstead, the mayor, stood outside wearing a look of satisfied excitement.

"I hear you got Carson!" he said. "What priceless luck!" He brushed past Price, who had to fight the impulse to throw him out. Shipstead grinned down at the wounded man. "So you outsmarted yourself finally, Will. I hear you tried to lay a rope on my new marshal."

"He's sure yours," Carson rasped. "No doubt about that now. Damn you, Shipstead, get outta here. I never fell for your smooth talk, and I don't have to listen to your sneering at me now."

"That's right, Shipstead," Price said. "He's a county prisoner, and right now I'm Jim Gantry's deputy."

"I know, and I've already wired Gantry to come and get him. But you'd better move him to the jail. You can't set here and let everything else go till Gantry gets here."

"Another matter I'll handle my way, Shipstead. Go on. He's in no shape to be ragged, even if I'd stand for it."

"All right," Shipstead said. "You've got him, and that's what counts." His good humor was restored by the time he had walked out through the doorway. Price locked the door, lost in deep thought.

"Carson," he said when he went back to the bed, "I'd like to know what kind of talk it was you wouldn't listen to."

"His wild yarn about makin' this town the cow capital of the intermountain." Will tried to rise again, then sank back. "What's the matter, Marshal? Don't he tell you everything?"

Price said angrily, "What makes you so damned sure Shipstead isn't telling the truth?"

"I've been sure ever since I found out he's got agents back east organizin' a big herd of settlers to come here."

"You found that out? How?"

"Seen a man in Cheyenne who heard some fellas beatin' the drum for this region back in the Iowa farm country. They've got a lot of fancy literature. They hold meetin's and give talks. From what they say, the railroad's even gonna give 'em special rates. That's why I'm buckin' Shipstead, and why he tried to frame me."

Price felt his cheeks begin to prickle with temper. If Shipstead was running a swindle on Snake Bend, he would have to fight his own town marshal. If the other cowmen knew what Carson did — as they must — it was no wonder there was so much tension here.

"You sure you can believe the man who told you about the agents?" he asked.

"I am. They'll be comin' by the hundreds and thousands

soon as the rails reach here. They'll cut up every piece of range in the country. They always do, then starve out, walk off and leave it ruined. And us ruined, too. But what're you pumpin' me for? You figure that makes you worth more money to Shipstead?"

Suddenly Price had no anger left against this man. "I'm pumping you," he retorted, "because I don't intend to ask Shipstead. Your sister must have told you about the men who tried to make off with her — Montana and Bronco Jack. You think the way she does, that they done it for Shipstead?"

"They're his wolf pack," Will said harshly. "When he found the cowmen weren't fooled by his fake stockyards and his talk of a cow capital, he decided to eliminate the leaders. They tried me, first, but I backfired on 'em and it was their man bit the gravel. Then they tried to railroad me, and I had to hit for cover."

"You don't know it, but Jim Gantry doesn't think you're guilty."

Carson stared up. "That supposed to make me happy about him takin' me to Baker if I pull through this?"

"It's only a statement of fact. The deck isn't completely stacked against you, and I think he'll give you every break he can. As I would if you'd trusted me more, if you'd met me somewhere instead of pulling what you did."

"The meetin' come off fine for you the way it was, didn't it?"

"You might not have got hurt if you'd just thrown down on me, then."

Carson snorted. "No, I'd just have got killed." The wound was thawing out, hurting now, and Price saw pain wrench through the other time after time. He got a glass of brandy and took it to Carson.

"Down it," he said, "then try to get some sleep."

Carson took the glass like a man hurting in every cell. He drank the brandy in thirsty gulps, then sank back, sighing heavily. He was too weak for more talk, and for a while stared dully at the ceiling. Then his eyes began to close. Price shaded the lamp and moved his chair over to the far wall . . .

Dawn washed out the darkness of his window until finally the oil lamp was pale and useless on the table. The town still slept, spent and inert after its payday orgy, and an hour past full daybreak the doctor arrived with Hester Carson.

She came through the doorway ahead of Doc Spears, all but running, to stand fixed and stark by Carson's bed. Price said nothing, moving back out of the way and watching her as the doctor, thin and gray, placed his bag on a chair.

Hester swung to look at Price.

"You worked it to perfection, didn't you?"

Doc Spears frowned and gently pushed her out of his way. She moved to the window, restless, filled with resentment and anger.

Quietly, Price said, "You credit me with more brains than I've got."

"Well, he's your prisoner now, and that's what you wanted."

"Is it?"

A little later, his fear was confirmed. The medico said with curt finality that it was out of the question to remove

Carson to Baker City immediately. The road was long and rough, the wound too close to the lungs. He couldn't even be moved to the jail for another day or two.

"He can stay here," Price said. He looked at Hester. "Would you like to stay and take care of him?"

She only nodded, her eyes hard and remote.

"You'd better see that Old Town understands he can't be moved," Price told Spears. "And get word to his friends."

"I'll see they don't try to spring him," Spears agreed.

Harris reported a little after seven, and Price left him on a chair in the hallway outside the door. He rapped on the door across until Sam Wens appeared sleepily.

"Sam, can I move in with you a few days?" Price asked.

"You didn't have to ask," Wens said and padded groggily back to his bed.

Price moved over what he would need, then went to the Empress and arranged for meals to be sent in to the Carsons. He had a cot brought up for Hester to use at night. Then he had his breakfast and went to a barbershop to get a shave. It was not until he found the shop closed that he realized the day was Sunday. The dawning stirred an idea in his mind, and he knew what he would try to do that day, when most of the town's establishments would be locked up.

6

Jim Gantry rode into Snake Bend around noon. After spending a little time with Carson, he came on down to the jail, where Price was killing time.

"Don't look at me that way," Price said. "I didn't know who he was till after I'd taken him."

"That's not the way Hester tells it."

"I know. She made up her mind I'm a Shipstead killer and doesn't intend to change it. That's a queer thing, Jim. Decent women think I sleep under a rock, while the other kind like the fact that I can get rough."

Gantry nodded, looking tired and worn. He probably had been in the saddle ever since receiving the mayor's telegram. He stretched out on the jail cot with a long sigh. "Older I get the less it matters to me whether a woman's decent or otherwise. So what's the difference? That's a wild lookin' little turkey you got on the door up there. Your deputy?"

Price nodded. "Best man I ever had working for me. Want to make him your deputy without pay?"

"Why?" Gantry asked.

"Sooner or later — and I think sooner — I'm going to lock horns with his honor. In which case, the county'll have to see that Snake Bend's a decent, law-abiding town."

"So catchin' Will got under your skin."

"A little."

"Good," said Gantry. "I'd like to hear your side of it."

Price explained what had happened, what Carson had told him later, and his own previous feeling that Shipstead, himself, was the main cause of tension and trouble in the town.

"He's got a legal right to turn this into a farm country if he can do it," Gantry said.

"But not to attempt murder on Carson or try to frame him," Price retorted. "He's got to be smoked out and made to fight in the open."

"How you gonna do that?"

"Know where he lives?" Price asked.

"One of the new hotels in Shippyville. The Oxbow. Why?"

"You go there and keep him busy for an hour or two. I want to take a look around his office."

Gantry lifted himself, swung his feet to the floor, grinning. "Good idea," he agreed. "If I don't come back, the coast is clear."

Price waited half an hour, then left the jail. He came up behind Shipstead's office building from the off-street side. There were no window blinds, and a cautious look through the glass showed him that the place was deserted. He tried the window, but it was fastened from inside.

Taking out his pocket knife, he opened the heaviest blade and set to work in the crack between the sashes. A little patience and he began to jiggle the catch around. In minutes he was inside the building, the window lowered quietly behind him.

He stepped at once to Shipstead's private office, which was hot and smelly from the entrapped air. All he hoped to find was some paper, perhaps a letter or an old check, that would help in what he hoped to do. He tried the drawers of the desk and ignored all but the locked one in the center. His knife soon had mastered its lock, too.

There was a clutter of papers in the drawer, which he leafed through swiftly. Nothing meant much to him, although it probably did to Shipstead. Then he saw something that interested him enormously.

It was a small, slick-paper booklet with an ornate engraving of a big, tree-shaded town on its cover. The title brought a brittle smile to Price's lips:

YOUR FUTURE IS WAITING IN SNAKE BEND

He knew he had found more than he had expected, a piece of the literature with which Shipstead's agents were flooding the farming country east of the Missouri. He shoved it hastily into his pocket, listened carefully for a moment, then left by way of the back window.

Within minutes he was in the jail again, immersed in reading the baldest piece of fabrication he had ever seen. The whole thing revolved around the thousands of fertile acres surrounding Snake Bend and just waiting for claimants and ploughs. It said nothing of dryness, sagebrush, raging cold and searing heat, nothing of cattlemen ready to fight for their range.

Empty land, the pamphlet said. Empty . . .

When Gantry returned, he took one look at Price and said, "I see from your face you had luck."

"How does his honor feel today?"

"Ridin' tall in the saddle. He wants Carson tried and hung as soon as he can get outta bed."

"Can he produce the two witnesses he'll have to have?"

"Yeah," said Gantry. "Says they been hidin' out in Horsehead Canyon ever since you run 'em out."

"Where's Horsehead Canyon?"

"Up-country. What you got up your sleeve?" Then Gantry answered the question for himself. "If they were killed or run clean to the border, the case against Will would have to be dropped. But we don't do business that way. Or do we?"

Price produced the booklet he had found in Shipstead's office. The sheriff read it with a darkening countenance. "Well, it only proves what a lot of people have figured already. What we gonna do with it?"

"Nothing right now. First we're going to cut the ground from under Shipstead. One way is to latch onto his two hardcases, ourselves. Then we'll give him the choice of fighting in the open or clearing out of the country, himself. Without his gunmen and the way this town's going to be after this literature is passed around, he might want to pack his trunk."

"He's a tough hombre," Gantry warned. "And so're them other two. Horsehead Canyon's an outlaw hangout. They've got friends there. Take a posse to root 'em out."

"I'll take care of them," Price said quietly. "Hester can still prefer charges against them for trying to abduct her. I was a witness. I'll bring them in, then we'll see if they wouldn't rather stay out of the pen, themselves. How do you get to Horsehead Canyon?"

Gantry told him, showing a growing excitement as he talked.

Price left town quietly and headed straight across country toward the Malheur, which he reached as the sun dipped toward the rolling horizon. He passed the mouth of a creek tumbling out of the hazy mountains to the north, but short of the town of Vale turned south up a lesser stream, into what appeared to be a vast and empty country.

The region seemed to be entirely without habitation, given over to loneliness and the wildlings among beasts and men. He did not want to approach the fateful canyon before night had fallen. Yet he wanted to locate it because he doubted that he could make out, after dark, the landmarks Gantry had given him.

He traveled at a lope that spared his horse, not pressing, loose and easy in the saddle. His guns rode in regular belt holsters.

He finally picked up horse tracks in numbers. They came in on a flat tangent from the north and indicated that he had cut a regular trail.

In the gathering dusk he rounded the point of a rim to come abruptly upon a band of sheep. Dogs cut loose with their barking, off to the right, where he saw the light of a sheepherder's camp. He deemed it wise to pause and determine what was there, and slanted his mount that way.

The herder was a hard-faced old man with a flowing, tobacco-stained beard, and held a rifle loosely. The noisy dogs fretted about the heels of Price's uneasy horse. The staring oldster ruminated, working on his chew, then spoke an order and the dogs quieted down.

"Howdy," Price said carefully, deciding he had best represent himself as one of the outlaws likely to be prowling out here. "I'm on my way to Horsehead Canyon in a hurry and kind of got turned around."

"Horsehead?" The herder's voice was gravel-throated. "That's only up the trail a piece. You pass that point of rocks up there, and the canyon comes in on the left. Know anybody up there?"

"I figure on getting acquainted."

"Better light down for a bait of grub."

"Thanks," Price said. "I hoped you'd ask. I haven't hankered to stop in any of the towns around here."

That and the two guns seemed to reassure the old sheepherder. Price swung out of the saddle, trailed reins and loosened the saddle cinch. The old man climbed back into his sheepwagon. When Price followed he saw that the rifle had been set down carefully, close to the stove on which a meal was cooking.

"If you don't like mutton," the oldster said, "supper's over."

Price laughed. He didn't like it but was hungry and made no comment. There were biscuits and coffee to go with the meat. They ate in silence; the tough old fellow seemed to have made all the conversation he was going to. Afterwards Price gave him one of his packaged cigarettes, which the herder examined with interest, then put in his shirt pocket, without comment.

Yet the old man kept studying him, Price knew. A kind of outcast, himself, he probably acted as an informal look-out for the outlaws in Horsehead Canyon, but Price meant to be there before the oldster could take a warning that a stranger was coming.

He rode on under the growing light of the stars. The air grew cooler as the trail climbed. Juniper stood at lonely distances above the sage, ghostly sentinels in the night. He recognized the point of rocks and passed it. Almost at once he observed on his left the yawning black mouth of a canyon. He rode toward it, entered a cluster of scab rock and pulled up to examine the foreground.

He would have preferred to wait a couple of hours to give the outlaws time to hit their soogans, but that would the sheepman a chance to carry an alarm if he felt inclined. So he rode on.

He progressed for perhaps two miles into the canyon, whose walls at first stood well apart. When the sides began to wedge in notably, his warning senses grew keen. Finally he stopped and concealed his horse in a stand of brush growing in the lower talus rocks.

He had worked a quarter-mile farther when he heard the metallic click of a gun being cocked. Just ahead the rock walls nearly came together, forming an easily guarded portal. Beyond would be the last reach of the canyon and the hideout. It was one of those mountain holes, Gantry had said, that often opened to form a retreat for men and horses. There was a sweetwater spring in the box end, and that was where the outlaw camp would be.

Price was moving so quietly he guessed the sentry had only been warned vaguely of some motion in the night. He halted with a held breath while his senses keened the situation, as he knew the sentry's were doing. The other man, he decided, was in the rocks on this side of the portal. He might have bedded down there for the night, but his uneasy vigilance indicated that badly wanted men were on up the canyon.

Crouched and partly moving on all fours, Price again crossed the bottom, then angled up the other slope. The strategy brought no challenge out of the night. A little later he crept around the side of a cooling boulder and saw below him a faint glint of metal in the starlight. Staring hard into the depths, he was able to outline the immobile hunkering shape of a man.

Price worked on with an Indian's caution and patience, using minutes, at times, to gain a yard. The night's business was too important to risk a struggle here, for any kind of warning might carry up the canyon. The pinching walls ahead began to force him lower on the talus.

He finally entered the narrow gap and slipped through, sharply aware that he was bottling himself up, if anything

went wrong. As he had expected, the canyon widened into
a box. Out of earshot of the sentry, he came to his feet
and hurried. He saw picketed horses, and counted six,
which made it possible that he had more men to handle
than he liked.

Beyond the animals he saw the camp, open and set
against the gully head. The sound of water came to him
faintly — the spring, he guessed. A tarp set upon poles made
a shadow in the starshine. He saw litter and, before the
tarp, flattened shapes that were sleeping men. He moved
to the canyon wall, coming upon the camp from the side.
His guns were out, his breathing alert and shallow.

Turning to the wall, he gave a muted yell, his cupped
hands forcing the sound against the rock wall of the canyon,
raising an instant echo on the other side. He saw men
rising from their bedding to stare instinctively first toward
the portal, then at the canyon walls. He counted five men.

He spoke quietly, incisively. "Company, gents — and
more than you can handle. There's guns covering you.
Better reach in the right direction."

Caught by complete surprise, they chose to obey. But
Price could feel his tension mounting. It was a hair-trigger
situation, and he didn't like the odds. He began to step in,
slow and wary.

"Montana!" he rapped. "You and Bronco Jack come
this way. Move, damn it! I'd as soon kill you — in fact,
sooner."

Montana was recognizable as he came in closer, and so
was the man who moved with him.

"Price?" Montana blurted. "What the hell is this? We
ain't been in Snake Bend since the day you told us to pull
out. What's eatin' you?"

"You haven't heard that Carson's there under arrest?"

"Will Carson The hell you say. But why come after us this way? We'll jump at the chance to go to court against that hombre."

"Maybe not." Price's voice was dry. "The rest of you men take it easy, now. I only want Montana and the coyote he runs with. I want one of you to go out and bring in three horses and saddle them. Try to make trouble, and I'll cut down any man I have to."

Somebody growled, "Curly, you go, and do what he says." A man responded, walking wide of the others. He took a rope off a saddle and went on. Price stood motionless until he came back, bringing three mounts, which he saddled hastily.

Price made his prisoners mount, then followed suit. To the three men on the ground he growled, "Start walking. You're going ahead of us till we're out of this hole."

They obeyed reluctantly. The movement brought the guard to this end of the narrow gut through the rock. He appeared openly, afoot, moved only by curiosity.

"Tell him," Price called to the outlaws ahead of him, "that somebody's a dead man if he doesn't throw down his gun and move away from it."

The sentry complied hastily. Price ordered him into the party and kept them trudging forward until they reached the place where he had hidden his own horse. He changed mounts, then told the four men to stand in the open until he could get his prisoners out of gun range. He was soon riding behind the two, moving swiftly down the main valley.

They had just passed the point of rocks when a gravelled throat roared out.

"Hands up, you hombres, and be mighty prompt."

Price was taken by surprise. Then he remembered the voice, and his shocked stare swept up to the rocks on his right.

The old sheepherder stood there with his rifle in his hands, its muzzle aimed at him, not covering the two outlaws. "Suspicioned you was a lawman when you went up," the oldster said. "An' I jest been settin' here waitin' for you to show back with some of the boys."

Price suppressed a groan. "What now?" he asked.

"We'll see when I get to the bottom of this. What's he want you for, Montana?"

"The hell with that," Montana answered. "You better kill him, Pete, while you got the drop. He's a fast 'un with them smokers."

Price had ridden with his guns holstered, knowing he could draw them in plenty of time if one of the prisoners ahead gave trouble. He knew there was no chance of beating the old fellow up there, with the rifle already trained on him. Maybe he was just a batty old sheepherder with a grudge against the law. If so, he was doubly dangerous.

"I'll help you boys," the herder retorted, "because my life won't be worth a damn if I don't. But I ain't gettin' no killin' charge against me. You two drag it, and I'll hold him here a spell."

"You're making a mistake there, too," Price warned.

"I'll be the judge of that. Go on, Montana. Rattle your hocks before I change my mind."

The two outlaws would have preferred to see the thing settled permanently, but were wise enough to take the break they had. They lost no time driving in steel, wheeling their horses and heading back up the trail.

There was nothing Price could say, and it seemed to him that minutes passed in stony silence before the old man spoke again.

"All right, lawman. I got nothing against you, but them varmints would have gut-shot me if I'd let you get past my camp with one of them. You kin drift."

Price rode on, anger roaring in him at first; then worry began to damper it. The wholly unpredictable upset had put the fat in the fire for sure. Montana would lose no time getting to Shipstead, now that he knew Carson was in custody. Shipstead would demand an explanation of his marshal's procedure.

The showdown with Shipstead, wholly unprepared for, was at hand.

7

HE REACHED Snake Bend at two in the morning, unsaddled his jaded horse, turned it into the Sundown's side corral without arousing the hostler and went on to the jail. Shorty Harris was there, canted back in a chair but fully dressed, with his six-gun riding its leather at his hip.

"Gantry relieve you?" Price asked.

Shorty nodded. "But there wasn't much need. This town's real quiet tonight. Mebbe I shouldn't of told you who the main troublemakers was. Might of dealt myself out of a job I like."

Price gave him a sour grin. "Snake Bend's not going to stay quiet, Shorty — quit worrying about that."

"Shomethin' new?"

Price was in no mood to explain, and merely said, "A town sitting on what this one does can't stay quiet long, that's all. You might as well hit the hay."

He had a bite to eat in the nearest restaurant and proceeded to his room. The door at the head of the outside stairs was now unlocked, and a lantern burned in the hallway. Jim Gantry sat by the door to the room that held Will and Hester Carson. The sheriff watched Price with unconcealed interest.

"You make out at all?" he asked, his voice held low.

Price shook his head, then explained briefly. Gantry shrugged.

"Well, you were on the right track," he said, "and we'll have to keep after them. If I could be sure they wouldn't show, I'd arrange a hearing before Judge Kerry for Will as soon as possible. Without witnesses, the charges would have to be dropped, and that's the only fair and decent thing to do."

"The next thing they'll do," Price reflected, "is get in touch with Shipstead. That's going to bring about the break, Jim. I gave that some thought riding in, and I don't think I want to quit being town marshal just yet."

"I'd rather you didn't, either," Gantry said. "But Shipstead controls the town council and can have you fired in a minute."

"Not when you think it over," Price rejoined. "That'd prove to the Old Towners and the ranchers that I'm not on Shipstead's side. Worse, it would give 'em a local deputy sheriff on their side."

"Mebbe that's what we want."

Price shook his head, fishing out his cigarettes and offering one to the sheriff. When they had lighted up, he said,

"The Old Towners still wouldn't be sure of me. If they could get rid of me, they'd put a man in my place they knew beforehand they could be sure of. The result here in town would be civil war, and it'd spread to the range sure as hell. I've got to stay where I've got the best show to stop that, Jim."

"You're right, I guess. So?"

"I'll just let it ride. Shipstead's going to hit the ceiling, but when he thinks it over, he's gonna see it like I do. How's Will?"

"Stronger," Gantry reported. "Doc says the worst is past and he can be moved over to the jail tomorrow. I hate to do that, but I can't stay here guardin' him, and you and Shorty can't take on the job, either. I tried to explain it to Hester, and she don't like it a bit, though I think I made headway when it comes to you. Got her to concede you didn't know who it was you were pluggin'."

"Thanks. Want me to relieve you here?"

"Just let me go down to the outhouse. You had a harder day than I did."

When, later, he let himself into Sam Wens' room, Price was surprised to find the gambler there.

"Knocked off work kinda early, didn't you?" Price asked.

He didn't light a lamp, for there was enough street light to let him see to undress. Wens' indistinct shape stirred in bed as Price began to tug off his boots.

"I knocked off on purpose," Wens said. "Had to see you and didn't know when you'd get back."

"Anything wrong?"

Wens didn't answer immediately. Reaching out to the stand, he took up a partly smoked cigar from the ashtray, struck a match and lighted the stub. The flame showed his face for a few seconds, and it was grave, strained and thoughtful.

"I've been having a little go with my conscience," Wens said. "If I've got one. Maybe it's only ethics. I don't like an informer, but which comes first? A man's loyalty to his profession, or his loyalty to a friend?"

"Sam, what do you want to tell me?"

Wens sighed. "It's not what I want to tell you but what I've got to, Mace. There's going to be a meeting over in the Great Western, Monday night. It's not supposed to be generally known, but the Old Town bigwigs and the leading cowmen around here are getting together."

"What about?"

"I don't know for sure. Maybe they think that when Will's strong enough to be transferred to the jail he'll also be strong enough to be freed by force. Or it could be they mean to get rough with Shipstead. What you gonna do if they figure the time's come to cut him down?"

"Then," Price said wryly, "I'd get the job of protecting him."

"And you'd protect him," Wens said. "Maybe that's why I'm going against my grain in telling you. Mace, you've got to be at that meeting and explain yourself to those people and try to win their confidence. I've tried, but I can't cut it by myself."

"Just tell me what room it's going to be in."

"I don't intend to pass on information," Wens rapped, "and try to keep it a secret that I did. I'll take you to that meeting and introduce you around."

"Sam, you're all right," Price said.

Wens only grunted, stabbed out the cigar butt and turned over, his back to Price.

In the morning Price dressed and left the room early, without disturbing Sam Wens. Stepping into the hallway, he found that Shorty had relieved Gantry at the post outside the Carsons' door.

"Had your breakfast?" Price asked.

"Yeah. All set. Gantry's out scarin' up the stuff to fix a cell for Carson."

Price descended to the street, into another sun-bright, hot morning. The business places along the thoroughfare were just opening to the trade. He had his breakfast in the Little Gem, and when he reached the jail Gantry was setting up a regular bed in one of the cells. From somewhere he had borrowed a screen to cut it from view out front.

"Spare stuff that belongs to the Empress," the sheriff explained. "No use makin' Will sweat it out on one of them damned jail bunks."

Price grinned at him. "I'm waiting to see his honor's face when he sees all these fixings."

"If you want a frank opinion, I'd like to turpentine his honor an' turn him loose to drag his tail across a lava bed."

Around ten o'clock they moved Will down on an improvised stretcher, got him transferred to the new bed and made comfortable. When he returned to his own room, Price found Hester still these, picking up and putting the place in order. She apparently had been startled to hear somebody coming in and, as he stepped through the doorway, wore a look of confusion. But she looked fresh and, in the soft, indirect morning light, even more appealing than the first time he had seen her, before the hostility had sprung up between them.

"Will you go home now?" he asked gently.

She shook her head. "I'm staying with Will. And you needn't try to talk me out of it."

"I wouldn't try, Hester. Let me arrange a room for you at the hotel."

"I can do that myself, thank you." Yet she stood with her attention moving across his face. As if somehow reached by his gentleness, she for the first time let her features soften. "It was kind of you to bring Will here and let me stay. I didn't realize at the time how much it was putting you out."

"That's all right. And you needn't bother fixing up. There's a woman takes care of this place."

For a moment she seemed hesitant, then said in a rushing way, "I rode over you pretty roughshod. Jim tells me I was wrong. I hope so. I want to think so."

"Then why don't you?"

She made a bewildered, slightly frustrated movement of her shoulders and head. "I trust Jim's integrity completely. I don't know if I can trust his judgment."

"By their works shall ye know them?"

"That's it."

"Jim thinks you're pretty special. I see that every time he speaks your name."

Hester Carson blushed.

She left, and Price for long moments was aware of her lingering presence in the room. He had lived long enough, known women enough to understand that where there could be an intense antagonism, there could also be an intense attraction. It came to him now that she had much to her that reminded him of Kitty Oline. It was an aspect in the relationship he knew he must not look at again. When he had taken up his crusade in memory of Kitty, he had put behind him the possibility of there ever being another woman like her.

Gantry pulled out for Baker City at noon. Though Will was past the need of constant nursing now, Price loathed the obligation to lock the jail when neither he nor Shorty was at the place. For that reason, he told Shorty to stick around, giving as his excuse the danger that Will's friends might decide to take matters into their own hands.

He did not go to see Bent Shipstead until late afternoon. Neither Montana nor Bronco Jack had come to town, but around three o'clock he saw a rough-dressed stranger step down from saddle in front of the stockyard office. There was a good chance that he was a messenger.

As soon as he saw the man emerge, swing up and ride out, Price headed down Utah. His heels thumped solidly; his jaw was square and hard. The office he entered shortly received him again into stale trapped heat. The same surly clerk was at the same inactive desk. From his startled interest, Price knew he had recently been the subject of discussion. His hunch about the messenger had been right.

The clerk started to rise, but Price's impatient motion waved him back. Beyond the inner doorway, Shipstead paced restlessly. As he came abreast the door he stopped, his body stiffening.

"Come in here, Price!" he said sharply. "I want to talk to you."

Price stepped on in, smiling in sour amusement as Shipstead carefully shut the door so the clerk could not hear what was going to be said.

"Let down your hackles and take a seat," Price said suddenly. "I'm going to do the talkin', you the listening. You made a big mistake and I'm here to warn you not to make a bigger one."

Shipstead's jaw slackened, his face grew bland and still. He swung over and dropped into the chair at his desk. Absently, he picked up a cigar.

"All right, start talking," he said.

"The first mistake was hiring me," Price said, "after I told you I would never enforce any one man's law. You wouldn't believe me. You had your own idea of gunslingers — your dead certainty they've all got a price. I told you I work for the town, not just one faction. That's why I went after Montana and Bronco Jack last night. It doesn't matter now that I slipped up. You've heard from them since, which proves they're not doing a thing without your orders."

"You work for the law, you say!" Shipstead retorted. "But you're doing your damndest to interfere with justice by removing the witnesses against Carson! Don't make your high and mighty talk to me, Price! I don't know what you're getting out of it, but it's something. You're pushing for all you're worth on the other side."

"You know better than that."

"All right. Keep talking."

"You," Price said, "had better be the one to tell them two so-called witnesses to call it off. You probably hate Carson, but revenge is all you could get out of crowding ahead with your frameup. If you still think it would get you the town, you're wrong. There's going to be a meeting tonight. And I don't think you'll like what that meeting will decide."

For the first time a hint of uncertainty showed in Shipstead's eyes. "How do you know there'll be a meeting?"

"Never mind that. I know. I mean to be there. And I'd like to tell 'em that the charges against Carson have been dropped. If I can't tell them that — well, next I think they'll take up the question of smashing your whole damned nester scheme. They might, anyhow. But it might draw off their steam a little if they could simmer down about Will."

After a long moment, Shipstead said, "The hell with you. I'm building a town here, and I don't see how I can be held responsible for the kind of people that are attracted to it. If nesters come, is that my fault?"

"Yes," Price said and reached into his pocket. "You won't admit it, but you probably wrote this beautiful little piece of literature." He held up the brochure he had found.

For a while Shipstead seemed not to breathe at all. The natural ruddiness of his skin lightened notably; his lips didn't meet.

"Where'd you get that?" he asked, at last.

"Illinois — Iowa — Missouri — it doesn't matter where, Shipstead. The main thing is that it's a dead hoax. It proves Will's right in what he's been claiming. It gives you a hell of a lot more motive for framing him than it gives him for killing your gunman. And if I pass it around at that meeting tonight, Shipstead, you might be swinging from a telegraph pole tomorrow morning."

"If I agree to get rid of the witnesses, do I get that booklet?"

"You don't get it under any circumstances. I'm just tellin' you it's time you got onto more solid ground."

"I'm on solid ground!" Shipstead said furiously. "There's

nothing illegal about promoting a town. Every territory in
the West has got its immigration bureau and promotion
agencies. How do you know this isn't good farm country?
I'm as honest a man as you are, and I'm not afraid of
the law."

"No. But you're plenty scared of the cowmen and what
they'd do if they saw this advertising. You better abate it
a little, Shipstead. Get hold of Montana and his curly-wolf
friend. Have 'em come to me and withdraw their testimony
against Carson. Then I'll make up my mind what to do
with this literary effort of yours."

Shipstead's features relaxed. "So you did come here to
trade."

"Did I say so? I'm only thinking about my job. I'd hate
to shoot up that crowd to keep it from turning Carson
loose. And I'd hate it worse if I had to do it to keep 'em
from hanging you. Which, if it reached that point, I
would."

"I know you're working against me," Shipstead said
bitterly. "That I can't fire you without handing the other
side a dangerous man. But I'm not taking your orders,
Price. Don't get that idea for a minute. Maybe I'll just
hand you the job of protecting me and let it go at that."

"You need to think it over more," Price said. He rose
and walked out.

He relieved Shorty Harris at the jail, told him to get
his supper and relax a while. Hester, he found, was with
Will behind the screen. He could hear them talking in low
voices, and wished he could tell them how far he had
stepped beyond the strict proprieties of his job for that
ephemeral thing called justice. Yet telling anyone could
defeat his ends.

Shipstead was a calculating man, cold as an Apache. He could be jarred, bewildered, thrown off stride, but his recovery would be quick. A man like that had a way of turning reverses into advantages — a calculating man who made use of everybody and everything that came his way.

8

SHORTY did not return to the jail until evening. He said, "Must be some more road herds close. Lots of cow ponies comin' in."

Price nodded, not caring to betray Sam Wens' confidence by revealing his knowledge of the coming meeting between the Old Towners and cattlemen.

"They all wear the same brand?" he asked.

"Wasn't close enough to notice."

"Well, if they came in quiet they're not so apt to raise hell."

"A cowpoke," Shorty said with some satisfaction, "is always apt to raise hell."

The news left Price uneasy, however — it could mean that the cattlemen had sent out word, and that the riders were in town to strengthen tonight's meeting.

Mebbe I can figure it out at the meeting, he thought. All the more reason I should be there.

Leaving Shorty at the jail some time later, he stepped out into the street. The sun, now behind the far Cascades, left the great desert in uncooled shadow. The breeze that rarely rested and never died was coming up a little, freighted with the smells of the outlands and their wild loneliness.

Shorty had been right about the cow ponies. He saw a dozen strung along the racks of Old Town, their brands miscellaneous. It dawned on him that it was the first of the month — ranch payday.

He passed on down Utah, continued through Cat Town, then came back for a tour of Shippyville. Without once losing his constant wariness, he was preoccupied with the question of how to approach the men he would encounter at the meeting, what he might say if Shipstead should call his bluff. He did not want to use the incriminating brochure, for that would almost surely lead to violence.

Sam Wens came out of the Empress dining room with the serene look of a man with a good meal under his belt. Seeing Price, he paused at the bottom step to apply a match very carefully to the tip of a fresh, black cigar.

Casually, he said, "Around eight. I'll be reading my paper out front at the Great Western."

"Sure," Price said and went on.

He had better than an hour to wait but needed it, having no idea of what he might do at the meeting beyond explaining himself and his motives and trying to make the cattlemen believe him.

He was standing on the corner of Second and Utah when a rider came rushing into town from the south. He whipped around the corner and pulled up before the jail in a flurry of dust, swung down at once and hit the board walk with his heels. Price turned that way at a half-trot.

Shorty had come to the door to fling a glance along the street. Seeing Price, he motioned for him to hurry. When Price stepped to the jail office, he got his first real look at the stranger, a middle-aged, nondescript individual in rough range garb.

The man said urgently, "You Price — the new deputy sheriff?"

"That's right. What's wrong?"

"Plenty. They need you up on Christmas Creek — real bad. Shootin' scrape. Man's holed up in a cabin, and he's holdin' a woman prisoner. She's done for if somebody don't take the reptile. He's loco — gone clean bad."

Price stared at the man in rising suspicion. It was a bad time for him to have to leave town.

"Who're you?" he asked.

"Pete Morse. I was ridin' in on the trail from Sheaville. Man stopped me. Told me to smoke in and send out the deputy. To Christmas Creek, he said."

"How far's that?"

"Must be twenty miles from here."

Price's penetrating study ran over the man, who seemed completely sincere. But after a hard ride he could seem so without being an actor. At worst, he could be the innocent tool of somebody trying to get Price out of town for the night. Or there could be a real, a desperate need for a lawman on Christmas Creek.

"Thanks," he told the man. "I'll take care of it."

The messenger shuffled out.

"Somebody could be setting a gun trap for you, Marshal," Shorty said. "Go easy."

"There's too much chance it's the real thing, Shorty. I've got to go."

"Send me."

"No. You stay here, and don't you let anything that happens in this town before I get back pull you away from the jail."

"You think they're set to spring Carson."

"Mebbeso. In which case you'll be in more danger than me. I'm banking on you, Shorty."

"You can, Marshal."

Price swung in swift strides to the livery. The hostler had been here for years, should know the country. "Know anything about Christmas Creek?" Price asked him.

"Sure. It's wild country. But some settlers have located there. Two-three families."

That explained the woman, and Price began to take the call for help seriously. He knew that much of the region south of Snake Bend was primitive, empty, the kind of country attractive to trail wolves. Some man like that could have entered the little settlement, started trouble. Settler men were not apt to be handy at gunfighting, whatever their courage. They'd want help. Their urgency would be high if one of their women were in danger.

"How'd a man get there?" Price asked.

"The Sheaville trail crosses Christmas Creek, mebbe twenty miles out. As I remember, them settlers are only two-three miles up the creek from there."

"Saddle my horse," Price ordered. "Be back in a few minutes."

He found Sam Wens steeped in his evening's reading at the Great Western. A copy of the *Oregonian* was spread before the gambler, a fragrant cigar rode between his fingers, and a glass of bourbon was close to his free hand. Wens didn't look up until Price slid into the empty chair beside him, then he frowned.

"Bad business, your coming here so early. If they get suspicious they won't let us into that meeting."

"We won't need in, I guess, Sam. I've been called out of town." He explained in a low, swift voice what had happened. "But I'd sure like to know what they do at that meeting."

"Sounds like the McCoy," Wens reflected. "On the other hand, how did they learn way off on Christmas Creek there's a deputy stationed here now?"

"They could have heard. Anyhow, I've got to go, Sam. Any chance you could attend that meeting by yourself?"

"I'm not playing the spy for anybody, Mace. You know that."

"Sorry."

"On top of that, it wouldn't do any good without you there to talk to them. I've already tried talk and didn't get anywhere. I think somebody's trying to tow you away from it, but I see that you've got to go. Watch yourself."

"Don't worry about that. Sorry again, Sam, and thanks."

"Why can't you send Harris?"

"Somebody would still have to stay and watch the jail. I still wouldn't get to the meeting."

"Then take somebody along."

Price shook his head. "I work better alone."

He stopped at the jail long enough to pick up a rifle and cartridges. His horse was ready at the livery, and he was soon riding south.

His horse, fresh and welcoming the chance to travel, ate up the miles. Hill after hill rolled before him, but the spaces between were wide and flat. The eternal sage of the intermountain grew thickly about him; lava rock made its upthrusts like scabs healed over great wounds. The last glow of dusk faded from the sky and night closed in. An hour past dark he came to the creek crossing the livery-man had described. Christmas Creek.

While the main road went on, a wheeled-out trail came

in from the right through close-hugging hills, following
the bank of the stream. Price stared that way in close
thought. More than once along the way he had ridden past
a place where there could have been trouble waiting. Yet
nowhere was danger so strongly suggested as it was by
that narrow road upstream.

He made his decision and swung his horse about. Back-
tracking for a quarter of a mile, he left the main road and
put the horse up a long sage slope toward the ridge to
the west. There was by then enough starshine for him to
pick his way.

He saw a winking light. There was no sound to disturb
the night's even tenor, certainly no shooting. He paused a
moment, realized that he had come down upon a place
where the creek gorge widened out into a little valley.
That was a cabin down there; he could now see a few
other buildings.

He kept to the ridge above the road as he went in, riding quietly. In a moment a dog's shrill, startled barking
rent the night. He saw a larger square of light next to
the small one. A man was standing in the doorway, and
Price called a hallo. The man held a rifle in his hand.

Coming up before the cabin, Price saw a bearded, burly
individual who wore no shirt. There probably were others
in the house, but they kept back.

"I'm the deputy from Snake Bend," Price said.

"So?" There might have been a little surprise in the
settler's voice; there was no excitement and no relief.

"Aren't you having trouble up here?"

"Not that I know of."

So — that was it. Price asked a few questions about the
neighbors. The settler had seen them all that evening, for

there had been a singing right here at his own place. A
woman had by then appeared, curious and reserved but
obviously not upset.

"Other cabins farther up?" he asked.

"Couple. Carmody's and Durnbo's." Both within a mile
or so."

"Thanks."

He rode on until he had passed the second cabin. He
had a mirthless smile on his lips as he left the canyon and
again climbed to the ridge. Certainly there was no captive
woman and besieged killer here, yet there could be something the settler might have know about without daring to
indicate the fact. He remembered the sheeper who had had
to live among outlaws; probably these isolated people had
to watch their step the same way.

Where the valley pinched into the narrow gorge, he
descended the slope quietly, getting down closer to the
creek. He judged himself to be about halfway back to the
main road when he grew aware of special interest in his
horse. He halted, stepped down, and moved to the animal's
head to keep it from making a whicker. Price stared ahead,
but could see only the shadowy darkness of the gorge.

They're there, he thought, and I'm going to find out
who.

He left his horse tied to a clump of sage, drew his guns
and went ahead on foot. Down close to the trail and the
creek he saw what had alerted his animal. Two other mounts
were down there, dimly visible in the brush. The whole
situation was at once apparent to him. Since the horses
had been left by the road, the men were east of them, forted
up near the road.

He kept on, skulking with slow care through the sage

and rock. Ahead and below the wasp-waist of the gully widened. At the narrows rock lay high on the slope. Men hidden there would have a clean shot at anybody coming alone the trail toward them. Price dropped flat, began to move with the greatest of care on a lowering angle toward the structure.

This brought him to a point that had far less protection than was afforded by the big rocks to those he sensed to be so near him. Yet he needed to be where his guns and voice could command the situation when he made his challenge. It was probable that there was a man on either side of the gulch, yet he could make nothing out in the darkness.

"On your feet, you sons!" he ripped. "With your hands up!"

He did not expect to be obeyed, and was not. Instead, a gun made a succession of red blotches below him. Lead shrieked and dug about Price before he fired. A man's high, wild, panicked outcry followed.

"Montana — for —" Then again silence.

In those few seconds Price knew whom he faced. He called, "Make up your mind, Montana! You can't go forward, backward, up or down without me dropping you in your tracks! Either you fight it out or give up! Which?"

There was no answer. A full minute dragged by. Price was patient. His gun reputation was of value only at a time like this — he let that reputation eat into Montana now. Bronco Jack had cried out like a man destroyed, and no other help could possibly come to Montana.

"It'll be the same three hours from now," Price called. "Get it over with. You've got me placed by now. Come up fighting, Montana, or with your hands in the air."

Then, at long last: "Price, you've got me! I'm quitting!"

Price saw the empty hands first, then Montana's head
and shoulders rising out of the rocks below him.

9

SNAKE BEND, at this hour of predawn, was darkened and
silent. Price rode along the street behind two horses, the
leader ridden by a subdued, disarmed Montana, the one
led just behind him carrying the body of Bronco Jack.
Montana didn't have to be told to turn right off Utah toward the jail.

Shorty Harris was awake, alert against the danger he
still believed might be present in the town. The wispy
deputy stood framed in the doorway, his hand on his gun,
as the horses stopped on the street. Then, recognizing Price,
Shorty relaxed, his features breaking into a winning grin.

"Everything all right?" Price called.

"Like a graveyard, Marshal. And it looks like you
handled your end."

Silent and subdued on the long ride in, Montana was
regaining something of his cocky assurance. He swung out
of the saddle as Price did. In the jail office he hauled
around.

"This ain't gonna do you no good, Price," he said. "What
the hell. Me and Bronco was just tryin' to catch ourselves
a little nap and we heard somebody yell to heist our hands.
Thought it was a stick-up. Bronco cut loose, and you killed
him. What you gonna hold me on?"

"Right now, armed assault."

"You can't prove it."

"We'll see."

Montana's voice turned wheedling. "Look, Price, we ought to talk it over. Even if you can prove it, what can you get me? Six months — a year, mebbe — up in Baker? That won't keep me from bein' the star witness against Carson, and he stands to hang."

"So I turn you loose?"

"That might be smart."

Price laughed.

He put Montana in the cell farthest from Will Carson's.

Shorty had left the remains of Bronco Jack at the livery and sent word to the coroner. When he returned to the jail Price told him he wanted the coroner's inquest on the dead outlaw held as early the next morning as possible. Then he went to his room and to bed.

He slept no more than two or three hours, awakening from habit with daylight. He rose at once, dressed, and tried to wash the sleepiness out of his eyes with cold water. He wanted to investigate the possibility that Pete Morse, the puncher who had brought the message to him from Christmas Creek, had spent the night in Snake Bend. If he could be found and made to identify either Montana or the dead man, he would be invaluable.

Price had a scant breakfast at the Golden Pheasant, then made the rounds of all the hotels. No register showed the name of Morse. He went nally to the livery and there, asleep in the hay, he found his man.

The puncher awakened with a start as Price gently shook him. He sat up, half angry, then, recognizing the man who stood over him, he looked interested.

Morse asked, "Did you get it salted down up there?"

"Yeah," Price answered. "Hell of a time to root a man

out, Morse, but I need you. Want you to take a look at a dead man."

The man's half grin left him.

The body of Bronco Jack had been placed in the livery harness room. The hostler unlocked the door, and Morse followed Price into the dark interior. There was a saddle blanket on the floor. Price opened the door wide to let in as much light as possible.

Morse stared down at the body on the blanket. "Who's he?"

"You never saw him before?"

"Not that I know of."

"All right," said Price. "There's a live one over at the jail."

Montana was still asleep on the bunk in his cell. Rattling the bars, Price roused the man, who sat up with a sleep-drugged glare.

"I've seen him," Morse said. "He's the man told me about that ruckus on Christmas Creek."

Price grinned. "Except it wasn't the kind of ruckus he told you. Morse, if you meant to ride on this morning, I'll have to hold you here. Want you for the coroner's inquest and grand jury."

Montana had by then realized that he had seen Morse before. The outlaw's cheeks sagged. He shoved to his feet with an angry swing of his body, stamped over to the bars.

"What's this?" he demanded. "I never seen that bugger before in my life."

Morse had a puncher's spirit; his eyes glinted. "The hell you say. What's he been up to, Marshal?"

"Used you tryin' to decoy me into a murder trap, that's all. Montana, the charge won't be assault, like I said. It'll be attempted murder. That won't get you any six months to a year, and you're as good as convicted, already."

"He's lyin'," Montana growled.

"Say that again," said Morse, "and I'll haul you through them bars and knock teeth down your throat."

"Want to make a statement, Montana?" Price asked. "To the effect that Shipstead decided it would be smarter to kill me than try to fire me? And, incidentally, that he's behind the false charge you brought against Carson?"

"I'm not sayin' a damned thing," Montana grated.

Price went out to the street with Morse, who was more than willing to hang around through that day. Knowing he could trust the puncher, Price thanked him. He went next to see Judge Kerry, the local justice of peace.

He returned to the Golden Pheasant for the rest of his breakfast and ate with relish. As soon as the barber shop was open he got himself shaved and felt restored. He had just stepped out to the street when the sudden sharp crack of a pistol shot carried across the town. He knew as the sound waves died that they came from the jail.

The back door of the jail was open, he saw, even as he noticed that Montana's cell was empty. Rushing on to the back steps he stared out into the weedy yard, to see Shorty standing over a flattened figure in the thin brush. Shorty's pistol was in his hand.

There was a look of guilty misery on the deputy's face. "Hell, Marshal — he said he was sick. Looked it too — dammit, I'm no doctor. But I guess I've got too cocky with this gun. I started to take him to the doc, and he made a run for it. I didn't figure to kill him."

The man face down on the ground was Montana.

Price stared at his deputy. "You didn't? Then your aim is bad. You got him dead center."

Shorty's face was a study in defiance and despair. "All right," he said. "Maybe I meant to kill him — hell, he crossed me and I got mad. Maybe I'm like you, Marshal."

The familiar anger rose in Price with a rush, and for a moment he wanted to blast Shorty in his disappointment. Something stopped him, something he had not known until today, that made all his yesterdays merge into a kind of haze he only half understood. The gentleness superimposing itself upon his violence surprised him — it was something he had not know since Kitty died — and it had something in it he had experienced yesterday when Hester Carson had withdrawn her animosity toward him.

He heard himself say, "Never mind — at least that's the last witness against Will Carson."

The two inquests were held that morning, and Morse's testimony made them a mere formality. Later Price went to see Hester Carson at the Empress Hotel.

"This clears Will, doesn't it?" she asked.

"As well as he can be cleared under the circumstances," Price told her. "I'll get hold of Gantry and the county attorney. Possibly they can arrange a preliminary hearing here in Judge Kerry's court. There won't be any witnesses against Will. The charges will simply be dropped — at least until there's some new evidence."

"I don't know how to thank you," she said.

Gratitude made her warmly beautiful, and once again he had the feeling that she might nullify the past for him — and knowing how completely he had been molded by that past and its bitterness, he almost felt fear.

He said gruffly, "Your gratitude might be misunderstood in some quarters, ma'am. I didn't set out to kill your brother's accusers."

She smiled. "I'm still grateful," she said.

He tipped her a brief nod and left.

It seemed to him almost fateful that when he reached the sidewalk, the first person he saw was Trixie. Her features brightened as she lifted a hand in greeting. He pulled off his hat as they came together.

"Long time no see," he murmured.

"Yes, darn you. Why haven't you been around to watch the show, at least?"

"Too busy."

She was deeply moved, maybe by this meeting, maybe by something more. She said in a rushing way, "I heard about you bringing in those men last night. One alive — the other dead."

"Both dead now."

"So I heard." When she saw he was anxious to move on, she added in a lowered voice, "Your latchstring still out, Marshal?"

For an instant Hester, as he had seen her a moment ago, floated into his thoughts. Then his jaw firmed.

"For you, Trixie."

Smiling, she went on.

The telegraph line between Portland and Salt Lake City was older than the uncompleted railroad. Its local office was in Old Town, and Price went there to send a wire to Jim Gantry. He had not met the operator — Oleson was a lean, sandy-haired man of indeterminate years, with a strong, honest face. When Price had filed his message and started away, the telegrapher stopped him.

"I got no business doin' it," Oleson said in a lowered voice. "But after what might have happened to you last night, it'd hurt my conscience worse if I didn't tell you about something, Price. That is, show you somethin'. Message filed here yesterday."

The telegrapher took a quick look at the window, then went over to his desk. He leafed through a clip of papers, found what he wanted and carried it back. Turning the file so Price could read it, he pointed, saying nothing more.

It was a penciled telegram, addressed to Doc Flood in Denver; "If interested in marshal's job Snake Bend wire immediately. Shipstead, Mayor."

It was not the message that surprised Price but the man to whom it had been sent. Doc Flood was known to every peace officer and gunfighter in the West as a killing machine, ruthless and without principle, who operated with equal savagery on either side of the law. The message had been filed shortly after his clash with Shipstead.

Price said, "Thanks. And I've never seen that message, friend. Don't worry."

"I am worried. This is going to be a ghost town if that son gets his way. I've been here a long while. I like it here. And I'm not one who thinks you're working for him — not after last night."

Price walked out to the street aware for the first time that he could be beginning to make himself understood by both factions in this town. Bent Shipstead might not have too easy a task pinning his badge on another man. Yet if Doc Flood hit these parts and went to work for Shipstead, even underhandedly, whatever he, Price, had accomplished so far might add up to nothing but danger for the community.

Thinking of Flood, he felt again the beginnings of violence surging to life within him — but wondered, too, how
long even he could escape the law of averages.

10

WILL CARSON looked better. He also looked hopeful. Price
gave him a guarded grin as he took the chair Hester had
used in this back cell.

"Heard the talk?"

"Yeah. It made good hearin'. How long'll it take?"

"I've wired Gantry. Considering his interest in your case,
I reckon he'll start at once, likely bringing the county
attorney. If it's possible to have your hearin' here, Kerry'll
accommodate them pronto. Sorry, but I'll have to hold you
here till that's accomplished."

Will looked up in surprise. "You think I mind after what
I was facin'? Price, I gave off plenty of head to you. I
was dead wrong, and I'm sorry."

Price motioned impatiently. "What I want to know is
what kind of man I'm turning loose. A ranny who's still
got a wild streak — or a man who thinks of his friends?
I can't help wonder what you'll do once you're outta here
and on your feet again. The Old Towners and cowmen
had a meeting last night. God knows what they might have
cooked up."

"I know about the meeting," Will said. "Johnnie Goodspear — he owns the Oxyoke — came to see me while you
were at the inquest, this mornin'. Harris let him in here.
The meetin' didn't get no place. Some was for busting me

outta jail. Some wanted to string up Shipstead and be done with it. Some argued against both, and nothin' got decided."

"I'm glad to hear that."

"Damn it, Price!" Will said angrily. "This ain't a case where we can just set around being orderly and lawful! Law an' order plays right into Shipstead's hands! Them rails are gonna be tied together in another month, six-weeks! Then — nesters! Hundreds of stinkin', range-ruin-in' nesters!"

Price reached into his pocket and pulled out the adver-tising booklet he had found in Bent Shipstead's office. He handed it to Will.

"There's black and white proof of what you've known only by hearsay, Will. It could be dynamite, or it could do you some good. Go to the railroad officials with it. It'll have to be the higher-ups, probably in Salt Lake City. Make 'em see what a stinkin' mess they'll be in two-three years from now if they don't do something to counteract this advertising and the work of Shipstead's immigration agents back in the farm country."

Will looked doubtful. "Yeah. But there's somethin' wrong with that. No railroad wants to talk itself out of a nice, juicy piece of business."

"Sometimes," Price admitted. "That's your problem. Make them see that they'll do just as well with cattle busi-ness. You can't stop progress, Will, but you ought to be able to bend it your way. Talk to your sister about it — talk to the other cowmen. They ought to be able to come up with some ideas."

Will plainly didn't want to accept the mission himself. He said, "Hester might do as well as I with the railroad — maybe better. And I might be needed here."

Price stood up. "Talk to her about it."

He left.

He found himself at loose ends, waiting for Jim Gantry to arrive from the county seat. This released his mind to resume its worry about Doc Flood, the gunfighter Shipstead hoped to bring in and foist upon the town as its peace officer. Flood's coming could mean but one thing — the start of a reign of terror and killing.

The day passed quietly, as did the evening. Hester came to the jail, and afterward Will told Price she was skeptical of the plan of showing the false advertising booklet to the railroad officials but was willing to undertake the mission. She would leave on the eastbound stage the next day. Price avoided the girl, not wanting to stir in himself things he sensed could change him — perhaps hurt him.

He went to his room around one o'clock in the morning, and it was not until he heard her light knock that he remembered Trixie. For some reason her coming failed to stir him. He had been sitting in the darkness, smoking, sipping brandy and thinking his long thoughts. He opened the door for her, caught the scent of her as she slipped past him, then locked the door again.

When he turned back he saw that she was standing close to him, expectantly. He remembered that she had come to him the first time after a gun fight. The night before there had been another — and here she was.

He touched her shoulder. "I'm glad you came, Trixie. I'm lonely. I need somebody to have a drink with me."

She stood very still in the darkness. He sensed she was studying him, trying to feel out his mood. He poured a drink for her, holding the glass up against the dim glow of the window. She took it silently.

"Have I made a mistake?" she asked finally.

"Lord, no. I've got the jitters. You're just right for getting me out of them."

"Do I start now?"

He did not answer. What was the matter with him? They were good for each other in a way that neither was for anyone else — but did it always taken violence to bring them together? He could understand her with his senses, but not with his mind, and this made him restless tonight.

He paced to the window, staring out. He heard movement behind him, and then her voice, speaking softly, and listened without turning.

She said, "I worried about you, even when I didn't know why. All I knew was that you'd gone out of town. When I heard what happened, I was glad that you'd come back. That you were alive. That you'd won. It made me feel — well, excited and alive myself, is the best way I can say it. I never knew anything could make me feel like this." She paused, seemed to wait. When he neither turned nor answered, she went on. "We're two of a kind, Mace. We don't need each other — except when we need to feel alive. You can't ever hurt me — I know that when you're done here, you'll ride away again. If you never come back — if you die — I'll just have lost a few moments I might never have had, anyway. I'll just never feel like this again."

He turned slowly, his restlessness gone. He realized she had gone to bed — he saw her dress dimly on the back of a chair.

He smiled in the darkness going toward her . . .

The first thing after his breakfast, Price went to the telegraph office, hoping to find word from Gantry. He learned that Gantry was already on his way, and bringing the county attorney.

The telegrapher looked at Price uncertainly, then said, "Flood got the telegram. He's interested. He's coming."

"Thanks," Price said and walked out.

At three Gantry rode in with the county attorney, who proved to be a young man, brisk, earnest and saddle-sore. Will Carson was able to dress and walk the distance to the little wooden structure on Utah where Judge Kerry had his court and law office. The hearing was quickly over, and from there Will went to Hester's room at the Empress, a free man.

Price and Gantry ate supper together in the Empress dining room. Later they climbed the stairs to Price's room for a talk. The brandy bottle was still half full, and Price poured drinks. Gantry disdained a ready-made cigarette and spun his own with a steady brown hand.

"You ever hear of Doc Flood?" Price asked.

The sheriff stared at him sharply. "Sure. What about him?"

"How long would it take him to get here from Denver?"

"Couple of days. Train to Kelton, then the stage. Why?"

"Then Flood's due to show here in a day or two."

"But why?" Gantry demanded.

Price gave him a bleak grin. "To kill me, likely. I tangled with Shipstead after you left. We had it out and he sent Montana and Bronco Jack to get me, and wired Flood to offer him my job. Must have thought at that time that his coyotes would be able to get me. Anyhow, I'm still here, and Flood accepted."

"Could he kill you?"

Price shrugged, "*Quien sabe?* He's fast, he's accurate,

and he's got somethin' left out of me. He doesn't care why
he kills a man."

Gantry didn't try to hide the concern he felt; he let his
brown, weathered face pucker with it. "What can you do,
Mace?"

"Nothing. I can't stop Flood from coming here, and I'm
sure not fool enough to try to run him out of town. When
he gives me a reason, I'll try to kill him."

Gantry suggested, "You and Shorty ought to whipsaw
him — be no more than right."

Price shook his head. "What makes you think that'd
work? He hasn't stayed alive up to now by accident. Besides, I've got to live with myself — the day I'm scared to
meet a man to his face, I'm done."

They were both silent a while. Then Price said, "Jim,
I'd like to ask you a question about Hester Carson."

"Go ahead."

"How is it with you two?"

Gantry made an embarrassed smile. "Pretty one-sided.
I popped the question, but she stood me off. Don't let that
get in your way, Mace. I got no claim to her."

Half angry, Price said, "Her deciding I don't sleep under
a rock doesn't mean she'll ever like me. Or even ought to
Having her kind of woman would make my whole life a
lie. Every man I've killed would turn into a ghost living
with us. And some day I'd want to stop a bullet."

"I know what you mean," Gantry said. "I've heard some
things about you — what made you what you are. Just the
same, you could quit."

"Not and face myself every morning."

Gantry asked, his voice suddenly low and kind, "Bother
you much?"

"That's hard to answer," Price said, tiredly. After a moment he added: "Guess not — as much as other things. How about a drink?"

They drank.

Gantry and his companion returned to Baker City the next day, the Carson case closed. On the day after, Doc Flood stepped down from the westbound stage.

Price, standing idly under the stage depot's board awning, said, "Hello, Doc. Long time no see."

"Why — if it ain't Mason Price!"

Flood, a big and burly man with brown hair that fell to his shoulders, let his gaze drop to the marshal's shield on Price's vest. His eyes — they were cold as polar wind — narrowed slightly. Shipstead's wire said nothing about the incumbent in the marshal's job. This was a deep-going surprise to Flood. Yet he said nothing, nor did he offer his hand since Price had made no such gesture.

Frowning, Flood walked to the boot of the Concord, moving easily for all his weight. He was handsome — a swarthy Bill Hickok, Price thought. Flood took his valise, then crossed over to the Empress Hotel.

Price put his mind to the fact that the day was Saturday, and the railroad payroll had come again. He made his rounds, his thoughts on each step he took. Shortly after five o'clock construction hands began coming in, and they soon swarmed over the town.

"We're gonna have fun tonight," Shorty told Price at the jail office.

"If you want to call it fun, go ahead."

"Matter, Marshal? You off your feed?"

"You ever hear of Doc Flood?"

"Yeah," Shorty said. "And that he hit town, today. But

he ain't scared me, Marshal, so how could he of scared you?"

"He's here to take over. Shipstead sent for him to be marshal."

Shorty stared at him. "How do you know that?"

"Never mind, I know. Forget it, Shorty, but watch your step with him. I want to handle him — is that clear? Leave him to me. That's orders."

"If you ain't gonna let me have no fun," Shorty objected, "I might as well let Doc Flood kill me. But I'll take orders."

Price laughed.

Snake Bend was roisterous that night, bawdy, but nothing blew up. Nobody tried to tree the marshal, and such arguments as developed were settled without gunplay. This at least was his night, Price thought, the kind of Saturday night he wanted for Snake Bend. The town knew precisely how far it could go, and had developed a healthy distaste for stepping beyond that limit. Price didn't see Flood again, and was able to go to bed by two in the morning.

He was at the jail office when, at eleven the next day, Shorty rushed in with his mouth hanging open in his excitement.

"Pinch me, Marshal," the deputy gasped, "to see if I'm still awake! I just seen Doc Flood at the stage depot. He's got his valise. I come by the Empress to see, and he's checked out. That man's leaving town."

Price's feet came down from the desktop and hit the floor. He stared into the gleeful face of Shorty.

"That man scared out!" Shorty chortled. "If he came here to brace you, he sure changed his mind!"

Price shook his head in bewilderment. It could happen

that Flood had changed his mind about wanting the marshal's job. Yet that didn't sound like Doc Flood.

Nonetheless, Flood left on the eastbound stage. Price wasn't there to see it, but Shorty watched. Afterwards the wispy deputy checked with the depot agent and learned that Flood had bought a ticket to Kelton, the railroad town.

"Now what do you think about that bugger scarin' out?" Shorty demanded of Price.

"He didn't scare, Shorty," Price said. "But I'd sure like to know what he and Shipstead cooked up. I can tell you this — we'll get another look at Doc Flood."

"Then we should of killed the son while he was here."

"I'm going to have to try, Shorty — before long."

11

ON THE following Wednesday afternoon, Price found himself in conference with Will and Hester Carson. Will was restless, Hester tired, depressed, almost apathetic.

Her report on her mission was brief: "Maybe you should have sent a thug with a club to pound sense into their heads. They were polite, aghast that their railroad could harm any section it passed through, and completely undisturbed by Bent Shipstead's promotion activities. They looked at his booklet, laughed and said it was a little fanciful but no worse than most of that nature. They see no reason why cattlemen and farmers can't live side by side like brothers, particularly when it would be very nice business for the railroad."

"They say anything," Price asked, "about when Snake Bend can expect train service?"

Hester nodded. "Some time around the first of October, they think, and maybe sooner than that."

Will whistled. "And every day's gonna turn the screw a little tighter. Well, Marshal, we tried reasonableness, and it didn't work, did it?"

"Not yet," Price admitted.

"You think it still might?"

Irritably, Price said, "It's got a better chance than un-reasonableness. You couldn't destroy the thing by killing Shipstead, Will, and his cronies on the town council, and all his backers in Shippyville who expect to get rich through the townsite. You can't shoot or chase off every nester that comes in after the rails, either. I don't think you could even get an injunction against the colonizing. The land's open to claiming, and you couldn't show in court it's not fit for that purpose — that's something only time can demonstrate."

"You sound," Hester said angrily, "like the bell of doom."

Price said, "Shipstead's got to be outsmarted. That's the only hope. You folks going back to Vale?"

Hester nodded. "Tomorrow."

Price had himself succumbed to her depression by the time he came onto the street. He was glad she and Will did not know about Doc Flood, or understand the man's meaning — yet through Flood some kind of showdown was bound to come. And if he survived it, there was always the chance for a break.

It was ironic that, rounding the corner of the telegraph office, he almost bumped into Bent Shipstead. A scowl leaped onto the mayor's face, and he walked stiffly, silently on. Price stared after him a moment, feeling his depression give way to the purposeful anger that so often drove him to action. Shipstead went along on Utah, heading back to the cattleyards. Price watched him out of sight, then turned and strode to the telegraph office. Except for Oleson, the operator, the place was empty.

Price asked, "Anything new?"

"Yeah. I took another wire to Shipstead a while ago. It went like this: 'Leaving 'Frisco with ten men. Pick up more in Portland. Dalles City in about ten days.'"

"Who signed it?"

"Flood."

Price could feel his jaw muscles pulling hard. He said, "Thanks," and stepped out onto the sidewalk in deep thought.

He found Sam Wens at the Great Western in his usual evening indulgence of reading the daily newspaper just in from Portland. Wens' natural geniality was on his face, his contentment with life as he found it.

"Sam," Price said, taking seat, "have you ever been in Dalles City?"

"Lived there a while, one time. Nice place. River town. Big shipping point in the steamboat days before the railroad come up the river."

"What's there that could cause a man like Doc Flood to stop?"

"Dunno. Why?"

Price knew this was a man he could confide in. He said, "You heard Flood was here? Maybe you knew Shipstead invited him. Well, he went from here to San Francisco. He picked up ten men there, and by now is probably on the train for Portland where he expects to pick up more.

They'll be in Dalles City in ten days. He's reporting to
Shipstead like I am to you. What do you figure it means?"

Wens was scrubbing his face with his hand, coming down
carefully over his luxuriant moustache.

"If Flood hired men in 'Frisco and Portland," he reflected, "they'd be gunmen."

"No doubt about it, Sam. Coming here. But stopping in
Dalles City first. Damn it, man, think. Why?"

"By God," said Wens, "the land office is there."

"That's it," Price said, but suddenly his voice was low,
tight. "Shipstead decided it best not to make two tries in
a row to get rid of me. He found another use for Flood.
He's bringing in settlers — suppose Flood left to hire gunhands who're goin' to homestead. They can fix it up all
nice and legal in Dalles.

"Dammit!" Wens said. "I believe you've got it."

"They'll serve as the nucleus of the nester colony," Price
went on. "Doc Flood with a big outfit of underworld thugs.
When the railroad starts bringin' in the innocents to be
fleeced, they'll be 'protected.' Sam, when the cowmen find
out, there's gonna be civil war in this country. Even Flood's
outfit'll be inside the law. The cowmen'll be outside if they
try to fight. And it'll be my place as a deputy to stand
against 'em."

The gambler had forgotten his newspaper completely;
his eyes were deeply troubled.

"You've got an alternative."

"What?"

"Get rid of Flood. If I know the kind of scum he's
probably picking up, they won't hang together without a
strong leader."

Wens asked Price to have supper with him, but he could

not bring himself to sociability now — he needed to be alone with his thoughts and surmises. He felt curiously helpless, playing this guessing game; he was not used to it, and the worry was strong in him that eventually he might be outguessed.

A perverse serenity seemed to have settled on Snake Bend. Price's work had become so routine that he was satisfied to leave most of it to Shorty Harris. He was aware also of a change in Shorty, himself. Regular eating had filled out his face, relieving its wizened look. Shorty had bought new clothes, boots and hat, kept shaved and barbered. He had begun to eye the girls in the town.

Although Price felt the other's past held pages best left unread, he trusted his deputy, and took the man into his confidence. Shorty took his reading of the situation seriously; he did not regard what was coming, this time, as fun.

He said, "By God — it looks like we're going to have to be the ones to start something to smoke them snakes out — just let me know when you're ready, Marshal."

Price did not see Trixie for days, and marked the fact. One evening, restless and unoccupied, he dropped into Gillette's Variety, ascended the stairs, and took one of the little boxes to watch the evening show. When her act came on, the same singing and fast-stepping routine with the same dapper man, she caught sight of him. Her glance came his way again and again.

She came up to see him afterward and, since the management required it, she had ordered a bottle of wine. Price paid for it. He gave her a cigarette.

"Things are dull," he said. "Damned dull."

"Aren't they? Maybe you shouldn't have run all the roughs out of town."

"Trixie, can't you ever want a man except when there's been excitement?"

She looked at him quickly. "I thought we were over that — I'm a woman who wants to be needed. Would you have had use for me?"

He could not honestly answer that, so he said, "Somebody else, other times?"

He saw the quick rush of color to her cheeks. "You know better than that. But you don't want to be obligated to me. I don't want you to be, either. There are times when we just don't mean that much to each other — you know that. But I'll know when you need me, and so will you."

"Trixie, you ought to have married. It's a wonder to me you didn't, instead of all this. You're thinking straight enough to hold a man."

"That takes two people's thinking — the man has to think straight, too. I'd be as bad for most men as you'd be for most women."

He knew that was true. They could neither of them face a lie, and both had gone beyond the point that, once passed, could not be passed going back. With him it had been when he cut down his first man from behind a badge that stood for personal vengeance — for the life he had lost with Kitty. The step he had taken then had been as irrevocable as a marriage vow; he had taken death as a mistress. What the step she had taken was he could only guess, and he realized with some surprise that he was not really interested.

"Want to see me tonight?" she whispered.

He shook his head.

Somebody paused outside the box. Price glanced hastily through the curtain, which he had left undrawn. Shorty stood there.

"Something, Shorty?" Price said, a little sharp.

"Yeah. There's somethin' at the jail, Marshal."

"You know Trixie?"

"Do now."

Shorty nodded slightly, and Trixie smiled.

The deputy did not speak again until they were on the board walk. "Said that to get you where I could talk to you, Marshal. That telegraph man — Oleson — was lookin' for you. When he couldn't find you, he stopped me. Told him I'd hunt you up. Might be important."

"Yeah," Price said. "Thanks."

The telegraph office was closed, but Oleson lived in back. He came to the door at Price's knock. "I'm gonna keep on till I get myself killed," he said nervously, "but I figured you ought to know. Flood's done his business in Dalles City. Be here in two-three days with twenty men."

Twenty men? Price felt as if his back hair had actually risen.

"The wire," Oleson continued, "come in just a while ago. I took it up to Shipstead."

"Thanks, Oleson. Don't worry about getting them on your tail. The thing'll break across this whole country soon as Flood gets here."

He went to his room, finding he was relieved to have the long and wearing inaction coming to a close. He still had no plan to pit against Shipstead's, but there was the chance for action now, and a man like himself to fight.

There were twenty-one men in the party that rode into Snake Bend three days later; Price counted them as they

came onto Utah from the desert road. Doc Flood was the
only one who seemed easily at home in the saddle; they
all looked at home behind guns. Price guessed they had
left the train at Baker City, the present railhead to the
north, and got horses there. Shipstead would be financing
them, and he seemed to have all the money he needed.

Flood rode at the lead with a kind of arrogant laziness.
They left the horses at the livery and tramped out onto the
streets of the town. But they hung together.

"Tonight they'll try to tree you and me," said Shorty,
beside Price. "That's the first thing Flood'll want to do."

"Mebbe not. They've got the law on their side, so far. If
Flood's not bright enough to want to keep it there, Shipstead is. No, it's two to one they'll outfit, tomorrow, and
then go homesteadin'."

"Seems a crime not to warn the cattle outfits."

"Don't you get ideas, Shorty," Price rapped. "If they're
asking for a range war, that means they're ready for it.
Right now, we're not, and neither are the cattlemen."

12

AT EIGHT o'clock, Hester Carson drove up in a hired buggy
and stopped in front of the Empress Hotel. Will came down
the steps, walking carefully, and they got in. Price, standing in the bay in front of the Snake Cafe, where he had
eaten his breakfast, put down the impulse to move over there
for a word before they left for home. Will's hotheadedness
would bring the trouble to a boil instantly — and so far
Price himself was only guessing.

He remained on the street thereafter, aware that Shorty was quietly drifting about. By ten o'clock, when a wagon came up from the construction camp, Price had seen neither Flood nor any of his men. Their horses, he knew, were still at the livery.

The wagon stopped at the corner of Utah and Third, then pulled over to the walk where it waited. The teamster wore a dusty gray shirt and overalls. He was chewing tobacco and looked tired. Finally Doc Flood came out oi the Oxbow Hotel, just off Utah, and crossed the street. He walked up to the wagon and said something to the driver, who shook his head. Flood stared frowningly toward the cattle yards and Bent Shipstead's office. He went back across the street and disappeared into the hotel.

Price moved down toward Third, aware that the driver was eyeing him with indifference. The wagon was light, its sides low, and Price's eyes narrowed when he saw the legs of what was obviously a survey instrument, together with some poles marked alternately white and red. He didn't need to be told there were probably sledges and stakes in the wagon, also, perhaps a tent or so and camp supplies.

Some locating was to be done, and the thing that astonished him was the fact that the railroad company apparently was to do the engineering work. Yet, on second thought, he acknowledged the reasonableness of this. The company was detached from the local trouble. It was their business to accomodate those planning developments based upon their own.

Price glanced down Utah to see Shipstead hurrying from the stockyard. Two other men accompanied him. Flood joined them on the corner of Third. The four climbed into the wagon, which started, turned into Third and drove into the desert.

Two hours later the gunmen brought in from the coast swung awkwardly into saddle and rode out in a group also, taking the desert road.

So great was his sense of impending violence that Price was surprised when the day ended quietly. The survey party and its armed escort did not return to Snake Bend. Shipstead rode in through the dusk and disappeared into Shippyville.

It was not quite ten, the next morning, when Doc Spears thumped into the jail office. The doctor carried his black bag; his frosty face was pulled into tight worry.

"They want you and me out at Oxyoke, Price!" he said urgently. "Arlie Tronson just rode in! There's been a fight!"

"A fight? Somebody hurt?"

"Worse than that. Johnnie Goodspear and Fred Halleck — both killed. Two or three more hurt."

Price was moving with Spears by then toward the livery, remembering that Johnnie Goodspear was the owner of the Oxyoke, up the Malheur.

"Might as well ride with me in the buggy," Spears said at the livery door. "Arlie went on back. Jake — my rig and damned fast."

The hostler, who had appeared from the barn office, whipped off into the dark interior. Waiting restlessly, the doctor continued, "Somebody tried to run a survey line through Oxyoke headquarters. That's what touched it off. Arlie said there was a couple of railroad surveyors doin' the work, with a bunch of gunhands backing them. I figured it was a matter for the sheriff's office."

They were soon rattling out the Vale road behind Spears' fast, light team of bays. The coroner knew the country and soon left the road, striking off across the rolling, sage-strewn terrain. At the end of an hour they came over a low divide to drop down into the river valley. Ahead Price saw the buildings of a ranch headquarters.

There was no sign of hostile activity when the buggy whirled into the ranchyard, but men grave, pale and tense stood about. "In the bunkhouse, Doc!" a puncher called as Spears jumped over the wheel, his bag caught up in his hand. The puncher took the team and Price stepped down.

Spears had already started to work on one of the three wounded men in the bunkhouse. Johnnie Goodspear and the other dead man, Price learned, were in the main house. The other riders told Price of what had happened.

The day before one of them had discovered some kind of survey party working toward Oxyoke from Eagle Point. They knew there was a benchmark up there, which sur-veyors always used as a starting point. But all through railroad construction there had been such parties in the country. It wasn't until they started working toward Ox-yoke that Johnnie went out to inquire about it.

"Fred — he's the other dead 'un," said a puncher, "went along. Rest of us was kind of watchin', and things got hot and heavy. First we knew, there was shootin'. We pitched into it but they drove us off. Then pulled out. The other boys got hit in that fight."

"Where are they now?" Price asked.

"Got a camp two-three miles up the river."

"Lend me a horse," Price said.

"You better take somebody along."

He ignored that and within five minutes was riding out, heading west up the river. The country was open, and he could soon detect a couple of tents. Most of the men were scattered and managed to look indolent and only mildly curious. Three men stood in front of one of the tents, Doc Flood and the railroad surveyors.

Price reached into his pocket and pulled out the deputy sheriff's badge, pinned it on. "That might not be news to you," he said to the surveyors, "although maybe it is to Flood."

Doc Flood had an amused expression about his eyes. "Mighty glad you come, Price. All we're trying to do is run a little survey. Them ringy sons started throwin' lead at us."

"What kind of survey?" Price asked one of the surveyors.

The man looked uneasy, and Price had a feeling that neither of them liked any part of this. The fellow shrugged and said, "All I know is I was told to help these people locate a tract of land."

"What kind of tract?"

"I don't know. That isn't my business. Bent Shipstead made the request and the engineering division of the railroad approved it. But I can tell you one thing. I don't think anybody knew it would lead to this."

"Nobody with the railroad," Price conceded. "But Shipstead knew it would, and so did Flood. Doc, I know you well enough to realize there's nothin' you wouldn't do for a fast dollar. But I also thought you had brains. You're tryin' to locate homestead claims for your gunhands, and it looks like you've picked the best part of the river valley. But I'm damned if I can see why you'd try to run a line

through Oxyoke headquarters unless it was to get your
gun work started."

"It happens," said Flood, "that Oxyoke's headquarters
are on public land. Johnnie Goodspear thought he owned
it, all right. But he never troubled to have a real survey
made. The land he homesteaded for his headquarters happens to be a few hundred feet farther south than he figured.
When I told him, he got rough and drawed on me. Didn't
he, boys?"

The railroad men nodded.

Price accepted that as fact. Goodspear probably had
failed to recognize Flood or he would have known that to
draw a weapon was to commit suicide.

"Probably," Price drawled, "you know more about the
survey, Doc, than the men here doin' the work for you.
What is it for? That's an official question you're going
to have to answer before a coroner's jury and maybe a
grand jury."

"Grand jury, hell!" Flood exploded. "We're completely
in our rights. We're a company, Price — the Malheur
Valley Irrigation Company. We're takin' desert claims
along the river we intend to irrigate. Twenty sections, running a mile on either side of the river and twenty miles up."

Price swore softly.

Flood grinned. "That's right. We've taken our land kind
of checkerboard fashion so's to make room for others we
hope'll come. She's filed on, Price, all neat and legal. And
the reason I'm glad you come out is that I demand protection, from here on, for my men. It's your place to provide
it, ain't it?" The eyes of the gunfighter laughed.

"Is Shipstead in this irrigation company?"

"That's somethin' you better ask him."

"And you're surveying the outside boundary lines now?"

"That's exactly it."

Price chafed at his helplessness. From his own previous guesswork, and the presence of the railroaders, he surmised that Flood was probably telling the truth and acting entirely legally. For the moment there was nothing he could do.

Curtly he said, "The inquest will be in town at ten tomorrow. You three be there, and anybody else that took part in the scrap." Swinging his horse, he rode off.

Prepared as he had been for the deepest kind of trouble, the extent of the scheme had staggered him. Under the Desert Act, he recalled, a man could take up a whole section provided he made some attempt to put it under irrigation. By filing on alternate sections along the river, the so-called company could control as much land again as it actually held by claim.

Not only had Shipstead set out to seize the whole main valley of the Malheur. He seemed to have destroyed the Oxyoke, already, and God knew how many others along the river. The other outfits might be luckier than Goodspear and own the land they headquartered on, but their open range was gone. They wouldn't wait to see that become effective. As soon as word of the Oxyoke fight spread over the range — Price didn't care to dwell upon what would happen.

Spears said he would remain a while at Oxyoke so, keeping the borrowed horse, Price rode back to Snake Bend. He stayed in the saddle when he reached town, riding on to the construction camp.

He made his way along the orderly, equipment-studded street, watching the tents until he located the office of the field engineer. There he swung down and, a moment later, was confronting the man, a stocky, youngish fellow.

"You've got some men working for Shipstead," Price said.

The man stared at him thoughtfully. "Shipstead — oh, yes. There was some kind of a little line he wanted run. I sent out a couple of the boys."

"A little line!" Price snorted. "Do you realize that two men have been killed over it already, and three more shot up?"

The engineer came forward in his chair at the pine-board table he was using as a desk. "You serious?"

"There's nothin' I'd like better than to tell you I'm not." Briefly, he explained what had happened up the river valley. "Sure. It's all legal. I know that. And the men who got killed and hurt probably started the fight. Just the same, I don't think I need to tell you that if the railroad backs that so-called irrigation company, it's gonna get the damnedest black eye any railroad ever had. Bent Shipstead's set out to grab off the best part of the Malheur country and turn it over to the nesters he'll bring in. The ranchers who're already here will fight 'em. If the railroad is against them, they'll fight the railroad, too. With guns."

The engineer said, bewildered, "But it's our place to help develop this region, Price. There's every reason to suppose this hot lava country, through here and over in Idaho, could be very productive under irrigation. Certainly somebody has got to try it to find out."

Price said, "Whatever the rights and wrongs are, it's criminal the way it's bein' done. The cattlemen's livelihood is being destroyed for an unproven experiment. But if you don't want to call your men off the job, that's your business."

"On the other hand," the engineer said tartly, "I'm calling them off as of now. I agree that it looks like a situation the railroad had better keep out of, entirely."

"Thanks," Price said and meant it.

He went to Judge Kerry's law office. By the time he got through explaining his business, Kerry's face was black with fury.

Price said, "I've got that survey stopped temporarily, though Shipstead's bound to hire some independent outfit to finish it. What can be done about tying it up legally—at least till there can be an honest hearing?"

"I dunno," Kerry said. "But I'll sure find out."

"And don't lose any time about it. Do anything you can to keep the thing hung up."

"What you going to do," Kerry said darkly, "about keepin' the ranchers from riding in on that outfit and getting slaughtered?"

"I don't know, Judge. I wish to God I did. But I don't know if anything can stop that after what's happened."

Kerry had already turned toward his law books, his usually genial mouth pulled long and flat.

Price found Shorty Harris at the town jail. Some of the anger was beginning to cool in him now, assume purpose. He explained to Harris, then said, "I figured the best place to hold the inquest is here in town," he said. "And Spears and Kerry'll go along with me. If we can get an impartial jury, Flood'll be bound over to the grand jury, sure as hell. Then I can hold him."

"First," Shorty said, his voice low and quiet, "you'll have to bring him in."

Price smiled bleakly. "A few days ago I was thinking twice about that," he admitted. "Now it'll be a real pleasure to try."

13

FLOOD brought his whole highbinding outfit with him when he came to Snake Bend for the coroner's inquest. They rode in arrogantly and went directly to the cattleyards, disdaining any doubt of their close alliance with Bent Shipstead. But they were not the first arrivals. Some two hours earlier the cowmen had begun to come in, not in one organized group, but singly and in small parties. By nine-thirty the town was loaded for an explosion.

Price, Spears and Kerry conferred in the judge's office.

"We don't dare impanel a packed jury," Price said. "If it was all Old Towners, a smart lawyer could use that to get Flood off, if he ever comes to trial. Draw half from Old Town and half from Shippyville, and you'll have a locked jury."

"Whom does that leave?" Kerry wanted to know.

"The construction camp. Plain gandydancers who don't have any kind of stake in this country. Neither side could kick about prejudice, and it'd stand up afterward."

"He's right, Judge," Spears agreed.

Kerry grinned at Price. "It's a little risky—nobody can guess at the verdict those gandydancers will bring in, and all hell's gonna pop if Flood ain't turned over to the county grand jury. Just the same, Price, for a walkin' thunderstorm, you've got a fair head on you. We'll take the chance."

The proceedings, held in Kerry's courtroom, were orderly. The jury drawn from the construction camp was a cross-section of that gentry, migratory workers, yet steady enough to understand the responsibility on their shoulders, and reckless enough not to be unduly cowed. The evidence was presented, the fact of two homicides established, with all pertinent testimony given. Out of it emerged a sharp picture of what had happened at Oxyoke, and salient in it was the fact of trespass, of a man's right to protect his own.

A puncher who called himself Bert Albright made a typical statement: "Hell, them hombres, without a by-your-leave, come onto Oxyoke like they owned it. I know Johnnie Goodspear only rode out to see what the devil was up. Of course, none of us could hear everything that was said. But I know there wasn't no advance notice that Johnnie didn't own the land they were surveyin', even though he thought he did. If Johnnie drawed first, which ain't been proved except by the other side's testimony, he was protectin' his property from trespass that was dangerous to him. And when Fred drawed, it was to side Johnnie."

The verdict carried the recommendation that Doc Flood be bound over to the county grand jury for further investigation.

Price stepped quickly up to Flood and said, "All right, Doc. Keep your hand away from your gun. You're going to jail."

The city gunmen made up about half the crowd in the room, the others were ranchers and Old Towners. The latter seemed to realize that any sign of jubilation would start instant and bloody trouble. Flood's henchmen shifted uneasily in their seats. Flood himself flashed them a restraining warning. He was not in sufficient danger to want a fight, not here.

He stood up and let Price take his gun.

Price moved quietly to the jail with his prisoner, and by the time they were off the street, Flood was smiling.

"You don't think I'll stay here very long, do you?"

"Not if you can raise bail."

"I'll raise it."

Price said very slowly, "Give me trouble, Doc, and you'll also have to raise a gun—against me. The law isn't going to shackle either of us forever."

Flood laughed.

Judge Kerry fixed Flood's bond at twenty thousand, as high as he could make it. Shipstead and the Shippyville business men put it up at once, guaranteeing his appearance at the next grand jury session in Baker City. Flood was out, temporarily a free man, by noon. He took his men and rode back to the survey camp up the Malheur.

Price went at once to the Great Western, where most of the Malheur ranchers had waited. He said, "Shipstead's bound to get the sharpest lawyers he can find, not only to defend Flood but to ram that so-called irrigation company through. But we've got them off-balance, stopped for a little while. Flood won't want to do anything that might cinch the case against him. The railroad isn't going to help them make their survey. And Judge Kerry is doing all he can to find out your rights. So I got to ask you just to keep on not starting trouble."

"That's mighty hard, Price," a man answered. "From the talk, them buggers have swamped the valley clear up past Vale. The Oxyoke, Mill Iron and Circle are cut to pieces the way it stands now. The rest of us have been chewed into.

We'll go, too, once the real nester flood is turned loose. Kinda hard to rest our case on the hope Flood'll go up for killin' Johnnie and Fred, that Kerry can find a way to set aside their land claims."

"Kinda hard?" somebody else exploded. "It's impossible!"

"I respect law," the first, a more moderate man, said, "but we've found out more'n once in this country that it can't always cut the mustard."

"So we got to run them damned dude gunhawks off!" the other shouted.

"That's what it looks like," the first agreed.

"Have you got men enough?"

"We got enough to tackle it."

"Half of whom you'd lose, sure as hell."

They were aware of that. Shipstead had drawn to the scene a fighting force sufficient to put it through. Technically he was within the law, so that he could call upon the forces of the county, the state, to protect him—as Flood had called upon Price for that protection, already. They knew that fighting could only guarantee destruction—yet they were fighting men.

Bent Shipstead was waiting at the jail office when Price returned to it. The mayor's face wore a black fury.

"I suppose you did your duty as you see it," he growled. "But it's the second time you've interfered with justice and meddled in my affairs."

"Ready to fire me, Shipstead?"

"No. I've wired Portland for more civil engineers. When they get here, I'll not only demand that you quit obstructing them. I'll insist that you give them decent protection or resign your deputy's commission. I'll demand Gantry's support or that he do the same—resign as sheriff."

"You're sure gettin' big, aren't you?"

"I know my rights. And you know your duty. Do it, Price, or quit so Gantry can appoint a deputy who will."

Price went to the telegraph office and sent a wire to Gantry in Baker City. There was a bitter frustration in him, for Shipstead had been right in his demands. It was not a lawman's place to weigh equities, only to carry out the law.

Judge Kerry was still poring over his law books when Price stepped into his office.

"Well, we done our part in the case of State versus Flood," Kerry commented. "It's up to the district court in Baker, now, and I wish it wasn't six weeks before the next session starts. But I'm glad it doesn't have to be handled here."

"Find any law on those desert claims?" Price asked.

Kerry's features darkened. "None very encouraging. Usually a claim's staked out before it's filed, and they're doin' it backward. But I dunno if that hurts 'em, as long as they filed the right descriptions. That oughtn't to have been hard. They're just helpin' themselves to a two-mile strip up the river from here."

"I've been wondering about that checkerboarding. That means every other section in their tract's still open, doesn't it? Why can't the cowmen file on 'em?"

"They've all used their preemption rights, already."

"But they've got punchers who probably haven't."

Kerry's eyes narrowed into sudden concentration. A faint smile broke on his mouth, but he didn't comment.

"I messed up Shipstead's timing," Price continued, "when I convinced him I was here to work for the law. Otherwise, he'd have had more time to get set before the thing broke into the open. The way it is, there must be loopholes he never got around to findin', at least to closing. I don't think

he wanted to show his hand till the rails were hooked up
and the main nester movement started. That way there
wouldn't have been any time to fight him."

"What good would it do to file on the alternate claims
through his tract?"

"It would save at least half of it. He'd have no place to
put more nesters, except on the fringes. To hold a desert
claim, you've got to irrigate it. And to irrigate the claims,
they'd have to carry ditch water to 'em. If their right of
way for ditches was cut up all along the river, they'd have a
mighty big headache."

"It's a move, anyhow, and by God we ought to make it."

"Why don't you go over to Vale," Price said, "and see
Will Carson? If they can scare up twenty men, cowmen
or punchers, with a right to homestead, they can make
a quiet trip to Dalles City and file. Ought to be done fast,
before Shipstead can scare up more men to do it himself."

"Then there'd be no need fightin' the survey he's bound
to continue with," Kerry said in appreciation. "The cowmen
would benefit from it as much as Shipstead, and Shipstead'd
pay for it. Price, you go a long ways just to keep peace in
your bailiwick."

"You're goin' to Vale?"

"Soon as I can hire a rig."

"Hope you can persuade 'em. I sure don't want the job of
protectin' that survey, and I don't reckon Gantry wants it,
either. Might as well make both sides agreeable to it."

Kerry grinned back gleefully. "They'll be agreeable.
They'd have done it sooner if there'd been any way to tell
where Shipstead was going to locate his nester colony. And
if they can knock it out of business they'll have protection
against it happening again."

Price, who was not given to self-admiration, felt he had done a pretty good day's work since the gunfight at Oxyoke. He could afford to eat the meal he had not had so far that day, and he went into the Little Gem for a steak.

The whole town, he observed afterward, seemed to have subsided into the lethargy that follows high tension. Snake Bend did its usual business, but it was quiet, slow-paced. By evening he was certain Shorty could handle affairs and went to his room, worn out.

Kerry was back to open his office promptly at nine the next morning. Price had been watching for him and went in.

"Men I talked to are taken with your idea," Kerry reported. "They're sure they can put it over. Will's back on his feet, and he'll push it hard."

Shorty came scuffing along the sidewalk and, seeing Price through the glass, turned in. His face was grave.

He said, "Marshal, Flood and his monkey menagerie is back in town. They all rode up to Shippyville."

"What next?" Kerry groaned, and his geniality was gone.

Price shrugged. "No law against their being in town, Shorty. And if Flood wants the whole of Shippyville, he can have it for all of me."

Yet Price was worried as he went outside with Shorty. A pack like that couldn't get their heads together without trouble resulting. Shorty went off about his business, while Price debated taking a stroll through Shippyville just to see what he could discover. He decided against it.

Jim Gantry reached town at noon. Price sat down with him in the jail office, making his report to the sheriff. Gantry's features changed to gravity, then lightened again.

"I think you found the way to keep the cowmen from committin' suicide," he agreed. "And I sure hope we ain't ever called on to furnish protection to Shipstead. Wouldn't you like to have a couple more deputies, just the same?"

"I'd like to have Shorty sworn in. But I don't know anybody else I'd rely on."

"Shorty's workin' for the county, then. And I'm gonna get me a good look at them gunmen of Flood's, then go through the wanted file when I get back to my office. A few of 'em must be wanted by some sheriff or police chief somewhere. While I'm here, I'll drop in on Kerry. See you later."

Price leaned back in his chair, lighted a cigarette and tried to relax. Fatigue was accumulating in him—strain was taking the fine elge off his nerves. That was bad. Doc Flood was being judicious about his conduct, yet he was an unstable man, wholly unreliable. He might go off his handle any moment.

The man who came into the jail office, a few minutes later, was from Shippyville—that was all Price knew about him.

"Price," he said, "the mayor wants you at a council meetin' they're havin'. He said right now."

Price stared for a long moment, then nodded.

He did not lower his feet to the floor for a long moment after the messenger had left. The city council met in a hall over one of the new stores in Shippyville but he had never had occasion to attend a meeting. He puzzled over the invitation now, but reached no explanation.

His entrance, when he reached the meeting, caused a stir. The mayor and his sycophants were seated about a big pine-board table at the deep end of the hall. The first two rows of the spectator chairs were occupied by Doc Flood and his men. The others were Shippyville business men, with a few hangers-on mixed in.

Shipstead could not conceal the glint of satisfaction in his stony features.

He said, "Sit down, Price. The council has just passed an ordinance you'll have considerable to do with. We thought it best to invite you here to discuss it."

"I'm here," Price said.

"Effective immediately," Shipstead resumed, "there will be no gambling or prostitution in Snake Bend. Such an ordinance is long overdue, but we've hesitated, doubting that you'd attempt to enforce it. However, these gentlemen here—" and he nodded at Flood and his men—"are starting farms in our vicinity and mean to bring their families here. The townspeople who have been kind enought to come here today are likewise demanding a clean and decent town. Have you any comments?"

"Just one," Price said. "You can't enforce an ordinance like that in this town, and you know it."

"You're the one who'll have to enforce it, Price. That's all, and thanks for coming."

14

GANTRY rolled a cigarette and took a long time between licking it sealed and touching a match to its tip. Even then the cigarette went out before he had inhaled a second time. The sheriff's seamy brown face was darkening steadily in the jail office light.

"It's not to make you quit," he said finally. "That'd put

you on the cowmen's side, with no badge to consider, the same as firing you would. And firing would be simpler and easier."

"He knows I won't quit," Price said "Shipstead also knows that as long as there's a anti-vice ordinance I'll enforce it."

"Or get yourself killed," Gantry said darkly.

"Exactly."

"Ah. That's it, all right. You might get the Old Towners to go along with you, but Cat Town—you'd put it completely out of business. That's what'd blow up on you for certain. They'll be done here when the rails join and the construction outfits leave. Until then they're coinin' money and they'll want to keep right on coinin' it, ordinance or no ordinance."

"I'm going to enforce the ordinance."

"I guess you got to," Gantry said. "But I'm hopin' that instead of a dead marshal, Snake Bend soon gets a new mayor."

"If it gets a dead marshal," Price pointed out, "it'll also get a new one. Ten to one, that'd be Doc Flood. With an impossible anti-vice ordinance still to be enforced. Doc'd go about it different from me. He'd go in shooting, getting rid of Shipstead's enemies in Old Town. Giving him complete control of the country."

"Want me to hang around a few days?"

Price said, "Don't see what good that'd do. You'll get word how I make out."

Gantry left for Baker City after swearing Shorty Harris in as county deputy.

Price entered the room of Sam Wens just as the gambler was getting dressed for the night. Roughly, he said, "Might as well go back to bed, Sam. You're out of business. The town just passed a new ordinance. No more gambling."

Wens' eyes went cold. "What's that?"

"You heard me. And there's another item, which don't concern you, but helps make things interesting. No more prostitution, either."

"You mean it," Wens said finally, "and you'll enforce it. By God, this is something. What's it about, Mace?"

"It's a way," said Price, "to murder a man and get applauded for standing for decency. Sam, I don't want to have to fight you or your friends, maybe kill some. But I will if it comes to that."

"How about Cat Town?"

"I'm goin' over to see Fink O'Toole. I'll tell him what I told you. But I don't think I'll get anywhere towards gettin' their co-operation."

"I don't either," Wens said promptly. "They'll defy you, and you'll have to close 'em up by force."

"Then I'll close 'em by force."

Wens shook his head. "I can't promise you much help, Mace—but I'll try to make them see you didn't ask for this. Maybe something'll work out. I'm a gambler, not a killer."

"Can I count on you?"

"I'll do my best. But Old Town's had Shipstead on their backs so long they've got saddle sores. Things might blow sky high."

Price found Fink O'Toole at the Big Tent. He declined the offer of a cigar and a drink.

"You won't like this, O'Toole," he said. "You got girls here who are hustling, and the council just passed a ordinance against it. Maybe that's every girl in the place—I don't know. But you've got to see they don't peddle it or get rid of them. That's final."

The veins in O'Toole's throat had swelled; his face was a fiery red. "Look," he exploded. "I went along with you, once. Now you're at me again."

"There's a new ordinance. I didn't ask for it and I don't like it. But it's there. On the books. And it's my job to put it in effect."

"I can't handle my girls!" O'Toole said, a little desperately. "All I could do would be to fire 'em! And that'd be goin' outta business!"

"I wouldn't know."

The Irishman's big fist hit the top of the desk. "Price, you've been around. You know them construction stiffs have got to have women they can get to or none of the decent women in these parts'll be safe."

"I know that. But there's the ordinance. It runs from one end of town to the other. It applies, and I've got to enforce it."

O'Toole said suddenly, "You tryin' to tell me somethin', Price?"

"I've told you. How you stay in business is your worry." He looked around the tent. "Place like this shouldn't be too hard to move, if it wasn't making money here."

"We could move outside the town limits." O'Toole glanced at him sharply. "Cost somethin', but mebbe better than fightin' a loco town government. Price, I'll see if the others'll go along."

"County sure doesn't care where you squat," Price said. He was smiling a little as he walked out.

He didn't encounter Shorty Harris until he got back to

the jail office, where he told his deputy of the new law. "You can quit as marshal if you want to, and keep on as a deputy sheriff."

"Why should I do that?"

"I don't know that Wens or O'Toole either one will get anywhere with what I suggested. If they don't—our jobs could be death warrants."

"You ain't quittin'."

"No."

"Then what makes you think that I would?"

Price grinned.

After six o'clock he came out of the Golden Pheasant, his supper eaten without appetite or taste, to see Fink O'Toole hurrying along Utah. The man had seen him and cut an angle across the dust of the street.

He said in a low, rasping voice. "I went around and explained. By and large, everybody in Cat Town thinks you been a pretty fair man for a marshal, Price. Trouble is, it's only two-three days to payday. We couldn't move that quick and get set up. And nobody wants to miss a payday. But Monday we move, or get started. Everbody's agreed to that. Meanwhile, we won't give you no trouble."

Price shook his head. "That won't be good enough, O'Toole. What you managers agree to won't be worth a damn when construction hands pour in with their pockets full of money and looking for what they want. You won't be able to handle your people."

"If it's peaceable," O'Toole exploded, "you don't have to look behind every door and into every bed to see what's goin' on, do you? That's the best I can do, Price. We start movin' Monday but no sooner."

"You know the ordinance," Price warned.

O'Toole shrugged and walked off.

The town was quiet again that night. There was no open gambling in Old Town. The parlor house on Idaho Street was dark. The word had got around, although there was every reason to suppose that, this early, the forbidden activities had simply gone underground while the situation was being digested, a decision made.

There was nothing in the Big Tent but sedate dancing. The cribs were lighted, but he saw no one coming or leaving.

It would be different Saturday.

Price had just had his breakfast, the next morning, and started for the barbershop for his daily shave when somebody hailed him from a back quarter. He swung about to see Will and Hester Carson on the other sidewalk. Grinning, he cut across, meeting them in front of the Rialto Hotel. They stepped onto the porch and took chairs. Price felt a lot better, not only at seeing Will back in business but at Hester looking so pretty and fresh—and friendly. They both were pleased about something, greatly pleased.

"It's done," Will said in a half whisper. "We had a meetin' Monday night, after I'd seen Judge Kerry, and the boys took off the next morning for Dalles City, goin' by way of the John Day to keep it quiet. They got there and done it yesterday. I told 'em to wire me here when they had, and Hester'n me just picked up the telegram."

"Good."

"What you think we ought to do next?"

"Let Shipstead find it out for himself."

"Mace—you've been marvelous!" Hester burst out.

Price's breath caught at the warmth in her voice and he snapped, "Don't get cocky!"

She wasn't to be put down; she kept smiling at him. "Me? I didn't have a thing to do with it. And the fact remains that Bent Shipstead's going to have a mighty nasty headache when he tries to figure out how to get the irrigation canals necessary to run his project with his right-of-way cut up by us."

"Shipstead's got brains," Price retorted. "Don't suppose he won't think of something to do about clearing his right-of-way—or at least make a damned good try."

"I'm convinced," Will said. "Plenty. And obliged to you. Oleson was tellin' me at the telegraph office that Shipstead's handed you a new one here in town."

"So to speak," Price agreed. "But I'm tryin' to hand it back."

The stage came rolling off the desert to the north and pulled up at the depot across the street. Price and the Carsons watched with the interest always engendered by such an arrival in a frontier town. Snake Bend's arrivals stepped down, others going south took their places, and the Concord rattled on.

Two men on the far sidewalk picked up their luggage and started off, looking as if they knew where they were going. Left were two men in corduroy trousers and jackets, high-laced boots and flat Stetsons. They stared both ways along the street, then started south on Utah.

A little later, Will said, "Goin' to our so called stockyards. Price, that's Shipstead's new engineers."

Price nodded. "I'm countin' on you to see that nobody interferes with their work, Will. The cowmen will want to hold onto their land claims, even if they can get the others vacated. And they'll want them surveyed. Let Shipstead pay for it."

"We won't butt in."

"Another thing I've wondered about, Will. Most of the ranchers in the valley have been running cattle a long while. Some of 'em must be pretty well fixed."

Will nodded. "I know. We've talked about it. This thing'll cost money before it's fought out. They're ready to foot the bill."

"I had something special in mind. I understand a land claim can be sold. I was just wondering if your people would have the cash in case some of Flood's gunnies lose their taste for homesteading."

Will's eyes kindled. "No doubt of it. But them buggers know Flood would kill 'em if they tried a double-cross."

"Flood might not always be around."

"Mace," Will said sharply, "don't get the idea you've got to brace that son for our benefit."

Hastily, Price said, "He's got a grand jury to face in another four or five weeks. With the thing tried in Baker, where Shipstead's got no influence at all, the outcome could very well be bad for Doc Flood. Get him out of the way, and Shipstead couldn't hold that gun crew together. He's smart, but he doesn't have what Flood's got. A cheap gunman— and they can be damned vicious—gets kind of hypnotized by a man of Flood's reputation. That's his main strength."

The Carsons left presently, riding back to Vale. Price walked the streets of his town, not that there was presently need of that but because he was growing increasingly restless. He tried to tote up the gains and losses of recent days, but the situation was too formless, as yet, too swiftly changing.

One thing was sure—the railroad was nearing completion. The depot being built down in Shippyville was nearly

finished. The rails coming down from the Columbia were
south of Baker City, now; those spearing out of the east
were an equal distance in that direction. Between, the new
grades and cuts were all but done, while the several bridges
needed in following the twisting Snake were about finished.
These were the slow things; the track laying would come
along fast.

And then?

Price shook his head doubtfully. The need for settling his
side of the dispute quickly and directly in gun-to-gun com-
bat was strong in him—even his own life or death did not
enter into it directly. Faith in himself and his mission had
become second nature to him—yet lives other than his
own might be lost if the issue were forced too quickly.
Particularly if he lost.

15

AT TWILIGHT on Saturday evening, Shorty Harris came into
the jail office where Price sat nursing his thoughts.

"Just been down through Cat Town," Shorty said. He
looked askance at Price as he got a drink from the water
bucket.

"How is it?"

"Gettin' yeasty."

Price nodded.

"When do we call their bluff?" Shorty asked.

Price stood and tried to stretch the tension out of his
shoulders. "Let's not crowd them," he said mildly. "How
about Old Town?"

"They seem to be playin' ball with you." Shorty sighed.

"That's why I like this town—or the one that was here before Shippyville and Cat Town sprung up."

"No harm in a town growing," Price reflected. "The railroad was bound to change things—probably make a pretty big place out of Snake Bend. All that's wrong here, Shorty, is that a little bunch of greedy men have set out to turn everything to their own profit."

Shorty rolled himself a smoke, then stepped out into the gathering dusk. Price followed a little later, but Shorty had already moved on around the corner of Utah. For a moment Price stood on the board walk, drawing in the night's warm, desert-scented air. Then he went over to Idaho and strode quietly up its length toward Cat Town. He stood on the edge of the clutter of tents and shacks, listening. The Big Tent was rowdy, all right, worse than it had been since his first clean-up activity. He had been obliged to crowd O'Toole too hard, or else the man's underlings were rebelling as railroad money began to flow freely.

He crossed to Utah, started back into Old Town and was halfway up the next block when a sudden series of shouts broke behind him. Swinging about, Price stared back into Cat Town. All at once a surging racket broke loose in the Big Tent. His boot heels started hitting the planks. By the time he reached the Big Tent's door, a riot was on inside.

Flinging a glance up the street, Price saw a slight figure racing toward him and knew it was Harris. He went through the door.

O'Toole faced him, and the Irishman looked frantic. "Dammit, Marshal!" he bawled. "It wasn't my fault! Some toughs come in here and started a fracas! It spread all over the place!"

Price let out a shout that was lost in the uproar, then waded in.

He had his guns out and was swinging their barrels. He heard Shorty's ringing, "Let's go, Marshal!" and swung a quick look to see O'Toole pitching in behind him, also, both meaty fists working. They waded into the brawling mob of construction hands and punchers surging over the big dance floor. Men went down and stayed down, and over against the sides of the place the dance girls looked on with mixed emotions.

Price fired a shot through the roof of the tent. The brawling men closest to him realized all together than a new, danger-ous element had entered the situation.

"Break it up!" Price roared.

Men fighting blindly, savagely, just because it seemed the thing to do, suddenly pulled apart and stood slack. Price sent a shot ripping over the heads of the others, and in a moment the riot was over.

"All right," Price said to O'Toole, "pick out the ones that started it."

The Irishman, raging and wholly on Price's side at the moment, swept his seething gaze over the suddenly sub-dued crowd. He walked down the floor a distance and looked about again. Shaking his head, he came back to Price.

"They dragged their freight," he said. "Started it, then skipped."

Price nodded grimly. "Never seen 'em before?"

"No. But they didn't look like construction stiffs or punchers, either one. Four of 'em in the bunch. Started to help themselves to the girls, and somebody objected. The rest was fast and furious."

Price took his time about answering. He looked at the
men still climbing groggily to their feet, and a few stretched
cold from his and Shorty's guns and O'Toole's sledging
knuckles.

"I'll let you try dancing again," Price said, finally. "Since
somebody seems to have used you. Next time, this place
gets padlocked."

The music struck up, and Price and Shorty stepped out
to the sidewalk. At that precise moment, two pistol shots
rang out.

They came from the cribs, a block over on a straggly
back street.

"Same bunch!" Shorty said tightly. "Be careful!"

"You come in from one end of the street, me the other,"
Price said.

"Good idea."

Shorty cut away at a bent lope, while Price moved the
other way. Rounding the lower end of the strung-out cribs,
he came onto the crude lane on which they fronted. He
walked into a hail of gunfire.

He was flat in the dust before the first crash of shots
died away. He had observed in that fraction of time that
the powder flashes streaked out from a slot between the
cribs. He held his fire, not wanting to endanger the girls
who must be cowering in the cribs, and also hoping that
somebody would think he'd been dropped permanently in
that first wave of lead. Up at the far end of the street,
Shorty seemed to be playing it with equal caution.

Four of them, O'Toole had said . . .

Price's patience paid off. He grew aware of a man
edging cautiously out from the corner of a crib. He fired.
The figure went down. His shot brought more gunfire from

farther up. He and Shorty laced into it together.

Climbing to his feet, Price went charging forward, his guns bucking. He guessed that there were at least twice four of the trouble-makers—probably a picked squad of Shipstead's gunmen sent out to kill themselves a marshal.

He found cover in the space between the two closest cribs, and the spasm of shooting died. He began to work between the cribs, until he saw the back of a man.

He called out softly. The man whipped around, shooting. Price cut him down. Somebody farther on let go a couple of shots just because there had been more shooting. Price reached the next slot, and the man there was onto him; he fired first.

They were body-shooters, like most of their breed, and the slug tore through Price's clothes. Te fired once. That brought silence.

He reloaded, began his stalk again. He wanted no prisoners, and they began to realize that. They were careful now of firing, of making any sound that would betray them —from hunters they had turned into the hunted. Women, close at hand, started screaming finally, their nerve breaking. Price sped through a slot onto Shorty's side of the crib row. Four men were streaking into the farther sagebrush. Price dropped two of them.

For a moment after the silence came he could only stand, breathing heavily. At last Shorty's tight voice ripped out: "Looks like we got it salted down, Marshal!" Shorty rose from behind a lava rock he had used for protection and came forward. "And it looks like they left a few carcasses for us!"

"That many less homesteaders," Price grated.

"It was Flood's bunch, all right. I figured that out from

the way they could shoot. How come you and me're still alive?"

"We're damned lucky, Shorty. Coroner's job from here on. Come on."

The fighting had energized the whole town, filled the streets. Quietly, Shorty said, "His honor is gonna get a jolt when he hears about this. He figured you couldn't tame Cat Town."

"Hadn't been for you and O'Toole, his honor would have had it just like he wanted."

There were plenty of people to help the coroner gather the bodies—there were no wounded. Six gunmen had paid the price of trying to set a murder-trap. The knowledge had its effect on Cat Town, even more than on the rest of Snake Bend. Somebody had tried to use its sordid reputation to cover a cold-blooded murder. Cat Town would from that moment back Marshal Price.

16

Price heard the knock, low and soft, and recognized it instantly. He had come to his room around one, as soon as it became certain Snake Bend would have no more trouble that Saturday night. He had stripped to the waist, was sitting in the darkness, his boots off, enjoying the night breeze that came in through his window. He held a glass of brandy, half finished.

Hearing the knock, he frowned.

He was half of a mind to ignore it, make her think he wasn't here. Yet she probably knew that he was, would be unnecessarily offended. He crossed over, padding silently, and opened the door. Trixie slipped through. He locked the door again.

"I don't like the way you come here," he said gently. "Can't you want a man when he hasn't just killed somebody?"

He heard her quick, sucked-in breath. "You've got the black mood again, haven't you?"

"Want a drink?"

"If that's all I'm going to get."

He poured another glass half full and handed it to her. This time she took the other chair, sitting sedately in the half-darkness. She sipped the brandy, accepted the lighted cigarette he held out.

"You think I'm twisted in my mind, maybe?" she asked.

"No. You explained it in a way the last time. I think you've lived too hard too long for your years. Variety halls, wild towns, one man after another trying for you. I think you're jaded, Trixie—that's all."

"I am. I'm jaded as hell, Marshal, and I wish I wasn't. Want me to go home?"

"Not if you need me."

"I did when I got here. I don't now."

"Sorry."

"No, don't be. It's time little Trixie took a good look at herself. Know what her real name is, Marshal? Alice—Alice Bowen. Her old man was a drunk, and her old lady ran off with somebody before little ol' Alice was old enough to remember her. What went wrong with you, Marshal? You didn't just start off killing people, did you?"

"I loved a girl, Trixie. Her name was Kitty."

"Nice name. Better'n Trixie. What happened?"

Price didn't answer that.

"Nice just sitting here once," she mused. "Not like—"

Somebody was hammering on the door. A voice yelled, "Price—you're wanted! There's been trouble!"

Price slid to the door and opened it. Stepping out, he pulled the door shut again to conceal Trixie. The man was one he'd seen around Old Town.

"What is it, fella?"

"Harris—he's shot—bad!"

It seemed to Price that the darkened hallway spun.

"What happened?"

"Flood shot him." The man was panting as much from the excitement as from running up the stairs. "Over in The Bank."

"All right, I'll be there."

Stepping back into the room, Trixie forgotten, Price began to dress. Slipping his guns into his hip pockets, he remembered her.

"Somebody plugged Shorty."

"I heard. Flood. Mace—are you going after him?"

"I'm going to see about Shorty. Be lots of people on the street. You better not try to go home just yet."

"I'll stay here till you get back."

Price went down the outside stairs two at a time. He'd had no idea that Doc Flood was in town, could not imagine what could have made him and Shorty tangle.

There was a knot of men outside the door at The Bank, and the interior was packed. Somebody had lifted Shorty onto a table, Price saw as he shoved through the press. The deputy was blood-covered from his belt to his neck and was unconscious.

"Anybody send for Spears?" Price rapped.

"He's comin'."

"What happened?"

The man he addressed had a visor on his forehead, wore black, sateen cuffs—a dealer. Price didn't care just then whether there had been a backroom game going on in spite of the new ordinance.

"Shorty comes in," the man said, "for a little poker before he hits the hay. But tonight Flood come in. Mean. Mebbe he'd just heard how his gunhawks got their tail feathers shot off in Cat Town. A little drunk, too. He started talking. About you, Price. Shorty—well, that little rooster got up and told Flood to shut his damned mouth. Flood reached and Shorty did—but Flood's Flood."

"He clear out?"

"You're damned right. Shorty's plenty good with a gun, but he ain't you, Marshal."

Spears came pushing in through the crowd, carrying his little black grip. He put his stethoscope on Shorty, lifted his eyelids to look at his pupils.

"He'll stand movin'."

"Not to his bunk at the jail," Price said. "Take him to my room."

He had forgotten Trixie until the men bearing Shorty on a door taken off its hinges at The Bank pressed into the room, but nobody seemed to notice her in the crowd. They got Shorty to the bed, then the doctor shooed them all out but Price. But Trixie was still there, over in the corner by the window. She was so unstirring she could have been a piece of furniture.

Spears was busy a long while with Shorty, giving him a hypodermic, examining the chest wound, then bandaging it. Afterward and as gently as they could, he and Price got Shorty undressed and under the covers.

The doctor said, "Not much more I can do right now, Price. He'll need somebody to look after him.

"I'll stay with him," Trixie said. "Please let me take care of him."

Spears looked around at her and smiled.

"How long you been here?"

"Came up with the crowd."

Spears knew better; he was also a gentleman. He nodded his acceptance of that, picked up his grip and went out.

Trixie came over to the bed, looked down at Shorty. She said, "That nice boy. Did you arrest Flood?"

"He lit out."

"I hope to God he's quitting the country."

"He isn't, Trixie. He got a little reckless, considering the charge hanging over him, but he won't run. That would be running from me. Flood's not built so he could do that."

"You'll go after him?" Again her face was troubled.

"Flood kind of made that my job."

He was satisfied to leave her with Shorty; it struck him for the first time that the real womanhood of her was aroused now. Or perhaps he just hadn't understood her. For once after a gun fight her feeling was for the loser, not the winner.

She hardly heard him when he opened the door and went out.

Price stretched out on Shorty's bunk at the jail and let the rage and the worry fill him. There had been gain in last night's insanity of violence, and he sought to weigh it.

Flood probably had devised the plan for getting him

murdered in Cat Town. Its backfiring in a way that had cost him six of his twenty men must have made him lose considerable face with Shipstead. That accounted for his coming into The Bank in a surly mood, mouthing his threats against the marshal who had so humiliated him. He hadn't understood Shorty or he would never have risked that recklessness. As a result, he had thrown the fat into the fire.

In spite of what it had cost Shorty, Flood's impetuousness had brought the break Price had hoped for when the outlook had seemed so black and hopeless. Instability could be a fatal flaw in a gunfighter.

He slept a little before daylight, then awakened and washed his face from the water bucket. Stepping onto the street, he turned up Utah, then into the alleyway to his room.

Trixie opened the door quickly at his low knock. Price saw at a glance that Shorty had regained consciousness. The deputy was actually grinning at him.

"This makes me think of when I used to set out in the hall guardin' Will Carson," Shorty said weakly as Price came up to the bed. "Used to be jealous of him having such a purty girl to nurse him. Never knew it could happen to me. Worth gettin' shot for, Marshal. Don't shed me no tears."

"So you were fool enough to cuss out Doc Flood."

Shorty looked hurt, "You should of heard that man give off head, Marshal. He called you a son-of-a—" The deputy looked at Trixie and broke off.

"I'm obliged," Price said, and dropped his hand onto Shorty's for a moment. "Trixie, you better go get some rest."

"I'm all right."

"I'll have a cot sent up and arrange for meals, then. Shorty, did you reach first?"

"No. I told him to shut his damned mouth, and he got busy. Then I had to go for it or get shot. And got shot, anyhow."

"I'm gonna get a warrant for him. Just wanted to be sure of the facts."

Shorty looked concerned. "Don't you go out to that survey camp alone."

"Maybe," Price said softly, "I'll let Flood come into town and give himself up."

"How you gonna do that?"

Price did not explain.

He got his breakfast, his usual shave. By then Judge Kerry had opened his office, and Price went in to talk to him. Kerry had heard all about Saturday night's developments and issued a warrant promptly.

Price said, "I'd as soon you let it drop around town that instead of me askin' for this you had to force it on me."

Kerry leaned back in his chair, nibbling on the pen he still held. He began to nod.

"Smart, Price," he said. "If Flood hears the rumor, it'll save you a trip out to his camp. He'll come to town looking for you."

"He's a vain man. If he's got to tangle with me, he'd as soon do it in public. Besides, he's got to save face with the rest of his crew and Shipstead."

"The word'll get around," Kerry promised. Not that I hanker to see any gunfight. I just don't want you goin' out there alone to make the arrest."

Price grinned thinly. "If you want the truth, Judge, I got no hankering to do that, myself."

He went from there to the stockyards and received some satisfaction from the uneasiness that leaped to the face of Bent Shipstead when he stepped into the private office there.

Without preamble, Price said, "Shipstead, you got any heirs?"

"No. Why?"

"Then this cattle yard and your share of the townsite will go to the state when you're dead."

"What the hell do you mean by that?"

"I mean some man with a decent interest in Snake Bend's future can buy it from the state. I don't reckon your Shippy-ville confederates will hanker to hang around after you're dead and buried. They'll sell out reasonable."

Shipstead made a pasty grin. "Your humor is very bad."

"You know it isn't that."

"So you're going to kill me. The great Price. I admit it would be easy. I've never been in a gunfight in my life. But that would be a little hard on your reputation, wouldn't it?"

"Maybe they'll just hang you, like they once wanted to, Shipstead. Before then I'll have quit my job. I won't have to stop 'em, and I sure don't hanker to."

Shipstead wet his lips with a quick tongue while Price watched him coolly. Doc Flood had been stampeded into recklessness, and he had better nerves than this man.

"Get out of here!" Shipstead grated.

"Not yet. I'm packin' the hardware here a while longer—till you're dead, one way or the other, and Flood's dead and his cheap gunswifts run off. And I want that anti-vice ordinance repealed, now. You thought I couldn't enforce it, would get killed tryin' it. You set the stage to make sure. Yet I enforced it. Old Town and Cat Town are behind me, now, and your damned ordinance won't get you a thing. So you better appease the citizens a little while you've still got the chance."

"The hell with you."

Price shrugged. "All right. Just remember that when the town blows up again, it'll be under you, not me."

He knew he had left a shaken man behind him when he walked out. But not a beaten man. Shipstead had gone too far; he had thrown everything into the pot, and he would fight to the end.

17

As Tuesday passed, Price grew increasingly aware that Judge Kerry was keeping his promise. The news about the warrant for Flood had spread through Shippyville, through Old Town and even down in Cat Town men watched Price wonderingly. The marshal did not do what they expected. His horse remained unsaddled at the livery; Price idled about the town.

According to the doctor, Shorty Harris had passed the danger point. Trixie remained with him steadily, and Price knew she was not working off any guilt complex in regard to herself. She had somehow been reached by Shorty's boyish helplessness, back in that first bad hour. She was showing herself to be what she had once said of herself— a woman who wanted to be needed.

Thinking of those two, Price walked quietly into Judge

Kerry's office. The justice tried to grin in his usual genial way, but his face showed strain.

"It worked better than I expected," Kerry said. "Even this town's started to believe you're scared of Doc Flood."

"I am scared of him."

"Well, I never did think you were all machine. I reckon Flood knows how scared you are, by now. Shipstead went up the Malheur this morning."

"I know. I saw him leave. Judge, don't make a fuss about this, now, but I got some money scattered in a few banks around the country. Since I've made good money and never had time to spend much, it's quite a little. I've got no heirs, and I never got around to making a will. It's something every man's got to do someday and most put off."

"You want me to write up your will," Kerry said gently. "Who you want to leave your money to?"

"Shorty Harris."

"I can write the kind of will you want in about three minutes. It needs a couple of witnesses. Go find men you can trust not to talk about it. I'll have it ready by the time you get back."

Price got Sam Wens and Doc Spears, and the will was signed and witnessed. Price knew that not a one of them would say a word about it afterward. They didn't say a word to him, either, about why he was drawing it up at this time.

He walked back toward the Great Western with Wens, who said as they strolled along the hot board walk, "Mace, why is it that we always believe in our hearts that the right is bound to win? I don't believe it in my mind, not any."

"It doesn't always win."

"You said it. But my heart doesn't agree. Does yours?"

"No. A man's heart is usually crazy."

"Crazy as hell," Wens agreed. "But I'm glad I've got mine, Mace. And somehow I want to say right now I'm glad I've known you."

Price grinned, but his lips were a little tight. "Thanks, Sam. And if all the towns I've worked in had had nothin' but gamblers like you, I'd have saved quite a little gun powder."

"How soon you think he'll get here?"

"Before sundown. He'll want good light."

Wens offered his hand and turned in through the Great Western's door. Price went on.

He had his supper at six, with two hours of strong light left in that day. His hands were steady, but he was too tight, altogether too drawn and edgy. He kept thinking of Wens, who lived by the cards, who made the law of averages pay off for him. Wens could lose, go broke, start over again. But a man had only one life, no more, and no place to get another.

He looked at his hands and was worried as to why he should have done that. They were still steady, with a will of their own to save him in a tight—instruments of trade of which he took the best of care. Half the time, in a fight, he never knew how his guns came into them.

He finished his supper and went out to the street, wanting a drink, wondering if a single brandy would be bad or good for him just now. He didn't have to decide the question. He didn't want to climb to his room for his own bottle, because he didn't want to see Trixie and Shorty again. For the same reason, he didn't want to go into one of the saloons. Almost he detested being on the street this way, with men covertly staring at him, wondering when he would get moving, what held him back.

At precisely six-thirty Doc Flood rode into town alone. He sat his saddle casually, looking indifferent as he came off Third, turned into Utah and went on toward Shippyville. He saw Price and Price saw him, but neither acknowledged that. The glances that came Price's way after that were a little scornful.

At seven o'clock, with better than an hour of good light left, a man came into the jail office. He looked frightened.

He said, "I was told to tell you this, Price. Flood wants to know if it's true you got a warrant for him. If so, he's at the Oxbow Hotel."

"Tell him it's true," Price said.

He stared at the door the man closed behind him going out. It was natural for Flood to want to make his play in Shippyville, among friends, but the insolence of Flood's challenge had set the methodical fury seething in Price again. It closed his mind to everything save the immediacies, weighing the situation and pondering its meaning. There was a chance that Flood had set a trap for him, and he sorted out the possibilities—a mirror flashed in his eyes, a sudden, untoward noise, an extra gun crashing out from a hidden place. There was no way of knowing what Flood would do, but the man had called for a showdown—and expected to win.

He looked over his guns, although he knew they were in perfect readiness. He smoked another cigarette, not because of his own nerves, but letting Flood stem his eagerness a little longer.

Then something came to his mind—the Oxbow was

Shipstead's hotel. Shipstead was a fighter of a kind, and
would go all out to win this fight, even to wanting to
supervise it in person. What this might mean Price would
have to go there to find out—but it was another factor to
keep in mind.

He started out, stepping quietly onto the street, seeing
its emptiness, feeling the warm touch of desert air on his
face. With only a cursory glance the other way, he turned
idly, strode along Utah. A moment later he was passing the
place where the first attempt had been made on his life
in this town. He remembered with grim irony that on the
night Ollie Kinkaid had emptied a shotgun at him out
of the darkness of this unfinished building, he had had
Shipstead's backing and Old Town's enmity. It was the
opposite now, and he liked this better.

There were four blocks, then, between him and the Oxbow, then two, and Price saw a lone man seated on the
hotel porch. There wasn't another person on the street. He
ran an expert eye over the buildings on either side of
the hotel and across the street. The three directly across
were one-story falsefronts with no upstairs windows, and
he was glad of that. But the hotel itself had two stories, so
did the building beyond it. And all of them had spaces
between them. He felt his breath running a little faster. The
man on the porch had stood up, was stretching lazily, was
looking Price's way.

It was Flood. Doc came to the top of the steps and
stopped there. Unlike Price, the man carried only one gun.
He was standing straight, staring earnestly toward Price.

Price started across the street. He slowed as he stepped
down from the board walk and looked across. There was
a window directly over Flood. It was open, and its curtains

were not blowing in the hot breeze. They were thick curtains, ones he couldn't see through, but they were not heavy enough to be so still . . .

Price called, "Flood, this is probably useless but I got to say it. I'm comin' over there to arrest you."

"What're you waitin' for, then?"

Price moved on. He had to watch not only Flood but that window above him. Maybe that distraction was the whole of the trick, but maybe not. Flood knew all about gunfighting. He'd been in a lot of scrapes like this. They were a habit to him, an addiction Price could see gleaming in his staring eyes.

For some reason Flood wanted to make his fight from the porch, not from the same level as Price's.

The edgiest man would make the first move; it was always like that. Price's feet kept pacing, a step from the edge of the walk behind him, two, three—four . . .

Price started action an iota of time behind Flood. Everything he had ever learned or planned or practiced went into it. His blurred hands brought the guns out of his hip pockets, but he had two places to watch.

His right-hand gun split the hot air with its crash; it sent a slug screaming and tearing through the right curtain of the window upstairs. The second gun fired at a lesser angle almost at the same time. Flood's gun roared and bucked. Its slug tore into the walk at its edge, well in front of Price, because Flood had triggered before the gun was lined.

Flood hadn't been able to line it. His knees were buckling, the gun fell from his hand and went hopping down the steps. The man went down flat on his back and lay still.

Price was still watching that window above. The curtain was now blowing inward on the breeze.

Price climbed the hotel steps, ignoring Flood after he saw that the man had a hole between the eyes. The lobby was empty until he rapped on the desk with a gun. A door opened, a man came out. He was pale.

"Which is Shipstead's room?" Price asked. His voice was low, soft.

"Nineteen. Upstairs."

Price went up the stairs, aware that his guns were still in his hands. But he didn't want to put them back, not yet. Nineteen was about where he had expected it to be, half down the upstairs hallway and on the street side. The door was not locked. Price turned the knob then gave it a hard, inward swing.

The door banged on the wall, but Price was staring across to the window. One curtain was still tacked down. So had the other been—once. A man lay on the floor by the window. A Colt .45, the same caliber as Flood's, lay about a foot from his hand. Shipstead hadn't fired it, Price found, but he had been ready to. A split second before Price did, ready, with nothing left but to pull the trigger. Shipstead hadn't been good enough, even then. Edging out behind that curtain to get a good shot, he had taken a slug through the right side of his brain, and loosened the curtain in falling.

Price walked out.

Shippyvillites still kept off the street, but it was a different story in Old Town. As Price came onto the street he saw men coming toward him. They must have recognized him, for all at once a shout rang out, then they hurried. Price's cheeks felt stiff and hard as they surged around him and went on to see the dead Flood. A fighter fallen. Evil as he had been, a kind of glory surrounded him . . .

18

Most of the rest of that night Price prowled restlessly. Jim Gantry came to town; other men spoke to Price. He was aware of answering questions, making his suggestions, but his senses were keened to the possible aftermaths of violence in a wild boom town that had suddenly lost its elected leader—for whatever his faults, Shipstead had been that. Almost anyone, now, was free to make a grab for power.

One of Flood's gunmen, a desperado named Curley Dawson, made an effort to rally the 'Frisco gunhands—Price marched him to jail and Gantry produced posters showing the man wanted in several states. That was the last show of force on the part of Shippyville homestead interests— by the time he turned in for a couple of hours' sleep at the jail, he was tiredly aware that all factions had agreed to a town meeting the following morning. Even the railroad was sending a representative.

By eight o'clock, the hour set for the town meeting, the hall over the Shippyville mercantile was packed. Old Town and the new addition were about equally represented, Price observed, while there were also a number of ranchers present.

A councilman rose and said briefly, "We agreed among ourselves to appoint Judge Kerry acting mayor, and he's accepted. So he'll take charge of this meeting." The fellow looked relieved when he sat down.

"There was a proviso," Kerry said, just as tersely, when

he had taken the floor. "I agreed to serve till an election can be held only if the council resigned. I'm happy to inform you all, I have their resignations. Meetin' adjourned."

"Now, wait a minute!" an Old Towner called. "What about that damned townsite? What about them damned nesters the railroad'll be haulin' in here any day now?"

"New meetin' called to order," said Kerry. "This time the first business meetin' of the Snake Bend Townsite Company, a new organization formed in my office today. Comprised of men with their hearts really in this town and country. Gentlemen of Shippyville, the company I represent is prepared to buy you out as of now. It's up to you whether you stay here and take a decent profit on your investment and improvements or go broke because nobody'll have a damned thing to do with you after the snake tracks you made among us."

"We'll sell," a man called from the Shippyville side of the room, and the others there seemed eager to agree with him.

"Meetin' adjourned," said Kerry.

"How about them nesters?" the first objector called again.

The railroad engineer got to his feet. He said, "Price asked me to come over and talk to you about that. I can't tell you that there won't be farmers coming to this country. There will be. But this I can tell you on authority secured from my superiors by telegraph today. The company will do its best to offset Shipstead's wildcat promotion. It will advertise extensively in the country where his agents have been working, telling the truth about Snake Bend. So I don't think you'll get a tenth of the farmers you would have otherwise."

"Which is all we can ask," Kerry said.

A murmur of approval swept through the hall.

Snake Bend actually needed no marshal during the quiet days that followed, but Price stayed until Shorty Harris was back on his feet. Then, in Judge Kerry's office, Price submitted his resignation.

"Wish you'd stay on," Kerry reflected. "Bringing you in was the one good thing Shipstead did for this town." Kerry shook his head. "Sometimes I think the man was more blind than crooked. He really believed in the law—his own kind. You cooled off more hotheads than one in this town—on three sides of the fence."

Price said nothing to that, except that he thought that was one hell of a fence. One part, Judge Kerry said, had been underground. Price thought that was pretty fancy language to use for Cat Town, the counterpart of which, one way or another, existed everywhere. He wondered silently whether either Flood or Shipstead, or any of the other men he had killed, were worrying which side of the underground fence they had died on.

After a while he went to his room and packed. Shorty had moved to the hotel. Trixie was no longer needed as a nurse, but the two saw much of each other. He got his saddle horse and loaded his possesions onto the pack pony that had carried them to Snake Bend. Trixie had quit the variety house. Price found her and Shorty sitting on the steps at the private residence where she now boarded.

Casually, Price handed Shorty his marshal's badge, saying, "You can turn the old one in to the judge, and he'll swear you in again."

Shorty stood up. "I don't like it, Marshal. But I don't reckon I can talk you out of it."

"The job's gonna be too damned quiet," Price said, grinning. "It's a job for a married man." For the first time he dared to look at Trixie, straight and deep into her eyes. She nodded, very slightly.

"Know somethin', Marshal?" Shorty was saying. "Her real name's Alice. That was my mother's name. I always thought it was the prettiest name there is."

Trixie looked as if she felt very happy that this was so.

Price stopped at Vale. Hester was at her little store but Will, she said, was out of town. "The ranchers are organizing to buy Shipstead's stockyards," she told him. "They want Will to run it for them. And there's more. Everybody thinks he's the one to go in as mayor. Judge Kerry doesn't want the job permanently."

"I know," Price said. "Tell Will I'm sorry I missed him and—so long."

She looked up very earnestly into his eyes. "There's something else I want to tell you, Mace. Jim told me about a talk he'd had with you. I agree with you that he's a fine man. I've promised to marry him."

"I'm glad. Luck to you both."

"And to you."

It was hard to end this last look at her, but Price did it. Rising to the saddle, he rode south.

Ford Pendleton is a pseudonym of **Giff Cheshire** who was born in 1905 on a homestead in Cheshire, Oregon. The county was named for his grandfather who had crossed the plains in 1852 by wagon from Tennessee, and the homestead was the same one his grandfather had claimed upon his arrival. Cheshire's early life was colored by the atmosphere of the Old West which in the first decade of the century had not yet been modified by the automobile. He attended public schools in Junction City and, following high school, enlisted in the U.S. Marine Corps and saw duty in Central America. In 1929 he came to the Portland area in Oregon and from 1929 to 1943 worked for the U.S. Corps of Engineers. By 1944, after moving to Beaverton, Oregon, he found he could make a living writing Western and North-Western short fiction for the magazine market, and presently stories under the byline Giff Cheshire began appearing in *Lariat Story Magazine*, *Dime Western*, and *North-West Romances*. His short story *Strangers in the Evening* won the Zane Grey Award in 1949. Cheshire's Western fiction was characterized from the beginning by a wider historical panorama of the frontier than just cattle ranching and frequently the settings for his later novels are in his native Oregon. *Thunder on the Mountain* (1960) focuses on Chief Joseph and the Nez Perce War, while *Wenatchee Bend* (1966) and *A Mighty Big River* (1967) are among his best-known titles. However, his novels as Chad Merriman for Fawcett Gold Medal remain among his most popular works, notable for their complex characters, expert pacing, and authentic backgrounds. A first collection of Giff Cheshire's Western stories, *Renegade River*, was published in 1997 and edited by Bill Pronzini.